This
Book
belongs to

_____

_____

_____

FIRE OVER LONDON

ERIC LEYLAND

FIRE OVER LONDON

London
THE BEAVER CLUB

THE BEAVER CLUB
*178-202 Great Portland Street
London, W.1.*

This edition 1957

*Set in twelve point Old Style
and printed in Great Britain by
Taylor Garnett Evans & Co. Ltd
Watford, Hertfordshire*

FOR
JEREMY

CONTENTS

	Author's Note	9
1	*In Which Visitors Come to Market Stanton*	13
2	*In Which Ezekiel Hewitt Seeks Assistance*	32
3	*In Which Tom Comes to Pudding Lane*	48
4	*In Which There is Uproar in Seething Lane*	69
5	*In Which a Pursuit Takes Place*	82
6	*In Which Tom Raynor Knows Both Hope and Despair*	99
7	*In Which the King Speaks and Tom Returns to Mark Lane*	115
8	*In Which the Admirals First Bicker and then Agree*	131
9	*In Which a Conspiracy is Revealed*	142
10	*In Which Tom Comes Yet Again to Pudding Lane*	156
11	*In Which London's Tragedy Begins*	170
12	*In Which the Wrath of God Descends*	185
13	*In Which the King has his Revenge, and Tom Raynor his Reward*	201

". . . . we to a little alehouse on the Bankside, over against the Three Cranes, and there staid till it was dark almost, and saw the fire grow; and as it grew darker, appeared more and more; and in corners and upon steeples, and between churches and houses, as far as we could see up the hill of the city, in a most horrid, malicious, bloody flame. . . . We staid till, it being darkish, we saw the fire as only one entire arch of fire from this to the other side of the bridge, and in a bow up the hill for an arch of above a mile long: it made me weep to see it."

Samuel Pepys, 2nd September, 1666.

AUTHOR'S NOTE

WE know that the Great Fire of London broke out at about two o'clock in the morning of September 2nd, 1666, and that it had its seat in the baker's shop of one Faryner, the king's baker, in Pudding Lane, near London Bridge. We do not know, however, the cause of the outbreak.

Faryner himself swore that his oven fire was drawn, that there was no draught in the bakehouse, and that thus the fire could not have started accidentally. Some support for this statement was forthcoming when a man named Robert Hubert was arrested upon his own confession of having started the fire by deliberately putting a fire-ball through the window of Faryner's shop; but though Hubert was executed, the occasion demanding a victim, it is quite certain that he was insane and had nothing to do with the outbreak. The court which tried him was convinced of this and did everything possible to persuade him to admit that he was lying in his confession. Hubert stuck to his story, however, and was duly executed. But the fact remains that we do not know the real cause of the outbreak.

In this book I have reconstructed the outbreak as it might have occurred. I do not say that it did

9

happen like this—but it could have done. There is nothing impossible about the theory, nor have I tampered with known facts.

One thing is certain—in our own age we have had great horrors fall upon us in London, but even Hitler and his bombers could not achieve such destruction as did plague and fire combined.

Eric Leyland

FIRE OVER LONDON

CHAPTER I

In Which Visitors Come to Market Stanton

"Away, puppy! 'Tis time this fellow was taught his manners! 'Death, would you have me run you through first?"

The boy flushed a little, for he was young enough at twenty-one to resent the assumption that this portly, rubicund gentleman, for all that he commanded an English fleet, could deal with him so easily. His hand went to his sword-hilt, but fell away again as he reflected that it was not desirable that in Market Stanton a Raynor should become implicated in a brawl. His family had been lords of the manor for three centuries, and though like many another estate in the England of 1666 the manor was now impoverished as a result of rallying to the Stuart cause twenty years before, Thomas Raynor was jealous of his family honour. It did not behove a Raynor to draw his sword in a tavern. Nor should youth brawl with choleric middle-age.

"I would but remind you, sir, and your friend, that having come to Oxfordshire to avoid the plague, 'tis foolish to accomplish death's work for him. You could have remained in London and died without trouble."

The speech was not calculated to soothe either gentleman's anger. Admiral Kenton's face grew even more suffused, both at the boy's impertinence

in presuming to offer advice and at the implication
that he had fled from danger. This, in spite of the
fact that with no official duties to hold him in the
capital he would have been a fool indeed to have
remained during the terrible summer of the previous
year, when near 70,000 people had died horribly of
the pestilence. His companion—who in twenty
years of association had been his friend and his
enemy in approximately equal proportions—let fall
an exclamation. He, too, did not take the boy's
speech kindly.

"By all the saints, I will deal with you, puppy,"
he growled, "after I have taught this fellow that
there is more to do at sea than eat and wine in
comfort."

Thomas viewed them both with some concern.
He had heard tales of their constant bickerings, but
hitherto had not witnessed any of the quarrels which
had enlivened the county since their arrival, with the
court, exactly twelve months since. When Charles II
had returned to London in February, five months
before, after a prolonged visit to the country,
Admiral Kenton and Admiral Cocker had
remained, moving from village to village, their
reputation going before them. Now had they reached
Market Stanton, and within an hour were brawling.
It was said in Oxfordshire that had their professional services been demanded now, for the war with
the Dutch, and that had they shown on their quarter-
decks even a fraction of the pugnacious spirit which
they had exhibited since leaving London, the enemy
would by now be laid low and not have ridden in
triumph on the narrow seas !

Thomas Raynor, riding to The White Swan courteously to make their acquaintance, had arrived to find them in the garden, excited hands clutching for swords. He did not know how the quarrel had originated, but evidently it was concerned with the sea and the fighting of men-of-war. The cause, however, did not interest him so much as the possible result of the brawl. He had heard tales of these incessant quarrels, but had paid little heed to them. As both gentlemen continued to live, and to live uninjured, he had assumed that the arguments were always settled without recourse to swords. Now, however, it was evident that they indeed intended to draw blood. Admiral Kenton, perhaps a shade more portly than Admiral Cocker, and a shade more choleric, had a determined look in his bloodshot eyes; Cocker, too, was in a fury, and both fire-eating gentlemen evidently intended to cross swords.

The boy, whose life had brought more responsibilities than were usual, was greatly concerned. Kenton and Cocker were made much of by the king, who ever liked buffoons about him; if one should be killed in this pleasant garden behind The White Swan at Market Stanton, there might well be trouble. Thomas Raynor, whose father had been killed at Naseby, ridden down by Rupert's first furious charge, had been head of the family all his life, and inevitably his outlook was different from that which would have been his had he lived the normal life of the son of a well-to-do squire. Now, therefore, anxious lest ill might befall Market Stanton as a result of the intended duel, he made one more effort to avert it.

He stepped forward, but before he could speak Cocker had jerked his sword from its sheath, and Kenton followed suit. The next instant, out there in the sunny garden, under the shade of the great trees which edged the smooth turf, the swords scraped. Tom stood helplessly by, watching the fight, which was notable more for its verve than its skill. If it had not been that the swords were sharp, and could kill—and that a killing might have unhappy results for the Raynors—the scene might have been comic. Both admirals were long past their prime, both had lost any suppleness which they might have possessed in their youth. Both were portly and choleric, both attacked with the obvious intention of ending the fight without recourse to the technique of the duelling-master, which no doubt they both heartily despised.

They were clad without attention to the fashions of the court, which dictated extravagantly curled hair, lace at cuffs and edges of breeches, brightly-coloured silk stockings, leather shoes and rosettes, being content with plain coats and unberibboned breeches, both garments stained and disreputable. Their hair was badly dressed, and they disdained the ringlets which Charles II had made fashionable.

As they furiously cut and thrust Tom could have laughed—had he not felt some responsibility for the affair. He had no interest in affairs of state, had no desire to go to court; but the king's displeasure was not to be lightly incurred, and his wrath might be visited upon the Raynor family if either of his favourite buffoons was killed, for Charles was an odd man and might decide to reprimand the head of the Raynor family for not preventing the disaster. And as Tom knew, the fact that he was the son of a man who had supported the martyred Charles I would have little effect. Generosity in the treatment of such families had been notably lacking since the restoration. The Raynors, like countless other families, had given their all to the Stuart cause; their reward had been negligible, and now they were impoverished.

Now Tom watched the cut and thrust with sinking heart. Why one or other of the old gentlemen had not by now fallen, he did not know. Neither had any defence worth calling by that name; both opened their guards incessantly. And yet no blood had yet been drawn. The boy was aware that excited faces were peering through the latticed windows of the inn as the duel proceeded, but his attention was too occupied with the event itself to wander to the building, so that the arrival of a second witness in the garden itself surprised him. He was even more surprised when he turned to find Dr. Samuel Chubb at his elbow.

"Why, 'tis you, sir . . . I did not know . . ."

The doctor, who as always was clad in the very height of fashion, as befitted one who owned a flourishing practice in London, smiled down at him. His lean, dark face, not unlike that of the king himself, showed no concern; his brown eyes were alight with humour as he glanced at the two admirals, whose breathing was now short and painful, and who were rapidly fighting themselves to a standstill.

"Ah, Tom, lad, I am happy to find you," he said. "They told me at the house that you might well be here. And I see that our firebrands are amusing themselves again."

"'Tis a strange amusement," muttered the boy. "Can you not . . . ? I would not have blood shed here."

The doctor's smile broadened. Negligently he swung the long stick with the gold knob which was the insignia of his profession, and moved towards the fighters.

"There will be no bloodshed, unless I bleed them both," he murmured. "'Tis not their habit to take these affairs too far. But, to satisfy you, lad, why, I will end it."

With that he strode forward. His stick swung up between the swords, and as Kenton and Cocker stepped apart, he stood between them, still smiling.

"Enough," he said pleasantly. "You will both presently have a stroke, and I am on holiday and do not wish to attend you."

Tom expected an explosion, but none came. Instead Kenton sheathed his sword, and Cocker followed suit.

"'Death, another moment and I would have had him," muttered the former.

Cocker growled an oath—but neither gentlemen showed any inclination to continue the argument. Dr. Samuel Chubb put an arm on the shoulder of each and drew them towards Tom.

"And now, let me introduce you before we sample the excellent wine mine host has in his cellar," he murmured.

"Excellent wine," spluttered Cocker. "'Tis the devil's brew and will bring you the plague!"

Samuel laughed. The wine his friends had tasted at The White Swan might indeed be devil's brew, but there was other liquor brought out only for special customers.

"I have some slight influence here," continued the doctor, "though 'tis entirely due to my friendship with Mr. Thomas Raynor, whom I now present to you. You must continue on good terms with him, gentlemen, and your stay at The White Swan will not be unhappy."

The two gentlemen grunted. Aware that their first reception of the boy had not been pleasant, they looked sheepish, but Tom was only too glad to find that his fears had been unfounded, and was courteous to them.

"My good offices are yours to command," he said, and was rewarded by low bows. The two admirals had never been known to offend—knowingly—anyone who could procure good liquor.

"Then let us drink," said Cocker, the formalities ended, "and Samuel, you shall tell us the news from London. We have it in mind to return. What of the plague? They say it has abated, but you can place no credence on rumour."

The doctor swung his stick. Glancing at him, Tom found it difficult to realize that this dandy had remained in the capital during the terrible year 1665, when London had been as a tomb, the living, the dead and the near-dead incarcerated within its walls, when horror had been piled on horror, when the death-carts had prowled the city without pause, laden with their cargoes of rotting death, when some men fell ill gradually, to lie in sweating terror for days, perhaps weeks, before the dreaded plague had taken them to the death-pits; when others, stricken suddenly, went mad in the streets, to fall dead within moments. This man had been his friend and before him his father's friend, and Thomas Raynor knew him as well as he knew any man. Yet even so he could not but wonder that Dr. Samuel Chubb, wealthy and his own master, had stayed in London, moving amongst the countless sick without fear, when he might have fled to the safety of the country. Many of his profession had done so. Sometimes it seemed but common sense to flee this death which no man could combat. Yet Chubb had stayed, nor did he parade his courage, but took it as a matter of course that a doctor should stay where he was needed. Tom found such courage difficult to comprehend.

"What of London, sir?" murmured the doctor. "Why, 'tis recovering. There have been few cases of the plague, and this is the time of the year when it strikes. And the Dutch, as you will have heard, have been driven from our coasts. We were threatened with invasion after the Four Days' Battle, but all seems safe now for you to return."

"Safe, sir? Do you imply that we . . ."

"I imply nothing, Edward," smiled the doctor. "An you desire a quarrel, you shall not have it. When I kill you, 'twill be with a smaller weapon than a sword. But my knife is as sharp."

At that Edward Cocker snorted but made no reply. Dr. Chubb attended both him and John Kenton, and with death the almost certain result of a surgical operation, the jest had not commended itself to him. Devil take it, he had not seen Samuel for nearly a year, and he must needs be morbid at their reunion! No man should make a friend of a doctor an he desired peace of mind!

"And you, John, have you had any more pain?" demanded Samuel, turning to Kenton. "Perchance you had better . . ."

At that Admiral Kenton exploded. He was of the same mind as his friend. Doctors were the very devil. Merely because a gall-stone had once been suspected—and the diagnosis subsequently proved false—was he never to hear the last of the fearsome subject of operations?

"Go to the devil," he growled. "You'll not cut me up, you rogue."

Dr. Chubb laughed aloud.

"We will leave you," he said, "to sample the wine. It is awaiting you. Mr. Raynor and I have matters to discuss. I have journeyed hither to see him. We will no doubt meet again."

He left the two admirals abruptly and, followed by Tom, left the garden without passing through the inn. The two fire-eaters watched him go with sour expressions. Who the devil did Dr. Samuel Chubb think he was, to take such abrupt leave of important personages? To . . . plague on it, to assume such airs and graces?

"Come, the wine," said Cocker at last, and would have entered the inn, had not an interruption occurred.

An ill-clad fellow in clothes which both gentlemen recognized without difficulty, sidled up to them touching his forelock. A thin, dirty face peered at them, hair matted above the forehead. He stood not more than five feet six inches, and could not have weighed more than ten stone.

"Your honours, can you spare a coin for a poor sailor?" whined the fellow, one hand already clutching as though at money.

Cocker stared at him. There was no doubt that he was speaking the truth regarding his profession. He was certainly a sailor.

"Seen your face before," grunted the admiral abruptly. "You know me, eh?"

"Yes, your honour, I know you. Best admiral the fleet ever had. Said so many a time, I have. Ezekiel Hewitt, your honour, served under you nigh ten years agone."

Cocker fumbled for coins and flung some down, not wishing to come in contact with the fellow, who might well be carrying plague infection.

"Never forget a face," he grunted complacently. "What do you here?"

"Been discharged, your honour, and not a penny I'm likely to see for back pay. Treat us like dogs, they do. Not like it was in your time, your honour."

Busily secreting the coins about his person, he leered up at Cocker, and then glanced at Kenton.

"Looking for honest work," he muttered. "They say there's a big house hereabouts. Would it have been the young gentleman you've been talking to?"

"If you mean does he own the manor, then he does, I believe," said Kenton. "And now be gone, fellow."

He jerked his friend's arm, and the two went into the inn. On one point they were agreed, and they

spent a pleasant hour over their wine vilifying one
Samuel Pepys, Clerk of the Acts at the Navy Office,
whom they characterized as a villain double-dyed,
a smooth-tongued rascal who aped his betters, and
was ruining the navy. There could be no doubt, they
agreed, that the pay rightfully due to sailors was
going into his pocket. It was a national scandal, by
the lord! A disgrace! The fact that they themselves
had grown rich by the simple expedient of pillaging,
looting and falsifying the accounts of ships under
their command, they did not mention. Samuel
Pepys should be hanged. Hanged, drawn and
quartered, in fact! The rest of the day passed in
unaccustomed peace. Neither gentleman knew that
Ezekiel Hewitt was to play an important part in
their lives during the next few months.

Tom Raynor and Dr. Chubb had no idea, either,
that the little man was to affect them greatly, and
being unaware of his existence naturally gave him
not a thought as they sat in the library of the manor
drinking their wine. They were concerned only with
their own personal affairs.

"You are as welcome to Stanton as the flowers
in spring," smiled the boy, regarding his friend
affectionately, "but I do not flatter myself that you
came merely to see me. What brought you, Sam?"

Dr. Chubb, whose name was inappropriate, for
it was apt to conjure up a vision of a corpulent
individual whereas he was tall, lean and debonair,
smiled as he sipped his wine.

"Then you do yourself wrong, Tom, lad. I came
to make sure that you were still alive—and to pay
my respects to your mother."

Tom nodded, but though he still smiled his eyes were sharp as they rested on the doctor's handsome face. This man was twenty-four years his senior, and had, in fact, brought him into the world. But for all the difference in their ages, they were friends; and never had there been a hint of patronage in the elder man's manner. Tom knew him through and through, and he was confident now that the doctor had not yet revealed his real purpose in making the journey from London to Market Stanton. But he knew, too, that he would not reveal it until he desired, and that no persuasion would affect him.

"My mother is well," Tom said, "as you can see." Then, correcting himself, "as well as she ever can be."

The other nodded. As a young man he had come into casual contact with John Raynor and his charming wife; and an enduring friendship had resulted. Then had come the great trouble, when England was rent in twain, when brother had fought brother and the king had been brought down. John Raynor had been killed, and his wife had never recovered from this grievous loss. She was in the world but not of it, and thus had been for twenty years.

"Yes, I know, Tom, and there is nothing a poor physician can do. Sometimes I wonder whether there is any disease we can cure. This accursed plague. Is it possible that it is indeed a visitation from God? Sometimes I think it must be. We doctors, we talk, and talk . . . and talk. The plague is caused by certain nitrous spirits in the air; in the spring, rains corrupt these spirits and they exhale putrefaction . . . so they say! But what do they—we—do?

Nothing, except to give drugs that have no effect, and poultice the tokens, again with no effect. I tell you, Tom, if you could have seen London last year! Every other door marked with the cross, the sick and the whole cooped up together, the very air heavy with death. And the death-carts . . . the accursed death-carts . . . bodies handed down from windows on hooks . . . and the death-pits. It was horrible, and I am not ashamed to say it though I have seen death countless times."

He fell silent, while through his eyes Tom saw the London of the great plague year. The vision conjured up, of those huddled, still mediæval streets, teeming with fœtid life, with evil death stalking them, was not pleasant And he could understand his friend's feeling of helplessness.

"Sam, do you agree with Dr. Hodges?" he asked. "It was he who maintained that nitrous elements cause the plague, wasn't it?"

The doctor stared at him and then laughed.

"Have you been reading medical treatises?" he enquired.

The boy looked embarrassed.

"A little. What of Kircher? He has talked of the plague being carried by little insects, worms, perhaps, that burrow under the skin."

Samuel smiled, and then rose to clap his hand on the boy's shoulder.

"So, you know of our Italian friend? Yes, I have heard of his theories. But Tom, no worms have ever been found."

Tom gazed into his glass. His imagination had been caught upon hearing an account of dead rats in London, of rats killed by the plague. They said these animals caught the disease from men; but suppose the rats gave the disease to men? The worms might come from the rats.

"I did not mean ordinary worms," he said at last. "Perchance they are so small none can see them?"

His friend turned away to hide his laughter.

"Nay, Tom, I do not think that possible. But enough of this. The plague has abated, disappeared very nearly. Nor do I think we shall have it again this summer. Already we are into August, and the weather is hot. Last year it was a terrible month. There is no danger in London. If I did not believe that I would not ask you to come with me."

"Ask me to come with you?"

Tom swung towards the doctor, eyes alight. He was fond of Stanton—nay, it was his life—but he was boy enough to yearn, sometimes, for more excitement than came his way in this sleepy Oxfordshire village. When the king had made his court at Oxford, Tom had often enough seen gallants and their ladies riding through Market Stanton; on several occasions he had offered what hospitality he could to some of the minor courtiers. The experience had whetted his appetite for the life and gaiety of the great world outside this village.

"Do you mean it, Sam? Would you take me to London?"

"Yea, and you will come. You are young, Tom, and this is no life for a youngling. Oh, I know that you have taken your father's place, and must be man before you are boy, but . . . take a holiday in

London, with me. The court is back at Whitehall. As you know, the king is gay. Fortunately, when he is gay, London is gay. This year they thank God that the plague has not struck and are gayer for it. You'll come, Tom?"

The boy was silent for long moments. From the time he could walk and talk he had understood that he was head of the family. He was the last of the Raynors, and he had quickly learned that, his father being dead, he and he alone must bear the burdens which civil war had brought to royalist families. Thus he had grown up serious for his age, and though in some ways the responsibilities had been to his advantage, for they had matured him and made a man of him, in others they had been to his detriment. He had known no boyhood. Stanton Manor and its impoverished estate depended upon him and upon him alone. His mother did not concern herself with the affairs of this world, but was at her prayers or in meditation all day. The restoration had brought no easement, for no reward for loyal service in the past had come to Stanton Manor. Only the great royalist lords had benefited from the restoration of the Stuarts. Tom had never been away from the estate for longer than a day and night.

"What of the estate?" he asked at last. "Somebody must be here."

"You have a bailiff, lad. Let him earn his keep. The estate will not vanish if you are away for a few weeks. Come to London, and I will show you the sights."

Tom fingered his glass and suddenly reached a decision.

"Yes, I will come," he said. "And you have my thanks, Sam."

The doctor grasped his arm.

"I would do well by the son of my friend," he said quietly. And then, with a quick smile, "you shall assist me in the writing of my book!"

At that Tom laughed. Sam's book! For eight years now, to his knowledge, he had been intending to commence writing a history of the recent civil war, and had even collected certain material, including papers and memoirs left by John Raynor, Tom's father. But of the book . . . not a sentence had been written!

Samuel winked and nodded. "Who knows, if the plague does not visit us again, perchance it will be written yet! Then 'tis a bargain, lad, and lest you change your mind, you shall come with me in two days' time. And Tom, do not misjudge the king, whom I hope you will see. He is no ogre—and would not have visited his wrath upon you had our admirals dispatched each other—nor is he entirely profligate. He is a shrewd man much beset. Parliament keeps him woefully short of money, and though he would assist you and others like you if he could, he cannot. Like other, lesser men, he is for ever poor."

He broke off as a servant entered the room. The man spoke to Tom in a low voice. Startled, Tom turned to his friend.

"Sam, do you remember Old Ben?"

The doctor nodded.

"Yes, I remember him, of course I remember him. What of it?"

He paused, for the boy's face was excited. Old Ben had served the Raynors for forty years, as boy, and man, and had fought at Naseby with his master. The latter had been killed, but Old Ben, then a man of sixty, had come through unscathed. Then, five years later he had disappeared. None knew the reason, but it was surmised that he had become embroiled in a quarrel with Cromwell's troops— they had at that time been quartered in the district— and had been killed, his body being disposed of quietly. Such happenings were not rare in those troubled times when England groaned under a military dictatorship. And Old Ben had a quick temper, as Sam remembered.

"Have you news of him, Tom?"

"Yes, there is news, or so says a fellow who is without. Old Ben! He used to play bears with me, Sam!" Then, to the servant, "Bring the fellow in. No, we do not mind his garments, nor his dirt, an he truly has news of Old Ben. Show him in, man."

The servant withdrew, to reappear in a few moments with a small, thin man, with a lean, dirty face. From beneath the matted hair two bright eyes darted about the room, finally to settle on Tom. Dr. Chubb viewed him with some suspicion, but Ezekiel Hewitt spared the doctor but a glance. He had no time to waste on one who was obviously but a dandy. In that assumption he proved his lack of judgment, but of that he was at that time unaware. He stared at Tom and then shuffled forward, touching his forelock with a dirty forefinger.

"Well, what news have you of Old Ben?" enquired Tom.

He was anxious for any word of the old servant, whom he remembered with love and affection, but this fellow's manner was unprepossessing enough to make him shrink away from too close contact.

"Well, what news?" he repeated.

Ezekiel hesitated. When at last he spoke his voice was whining.

"Give a poor sailor a bite to eat and a drink, your honour," he muttered. "Come a long way with the message, I have. Poor Ben, a good man he was and asked me on his death-bed to come to you."

"You shall eat and drink and welcome, an you speak the truth," said the boy.

"Well, your honour, it was like this. Came up alongside Old Ben I did in London not six months ago. Treated me kindly, he did, being as I was a sailor what couldn't get any money out of the Navy Office, rot 'em. Then he was taken with the plague, and when he was dying he asked me to come to you here and remember him kindly to you. Said you might give me work, your honour. Handy man I am. I can cook and sew and make myself useful. All I need is a clean up and some food in my belly."

Tom gazed out of the window across the smooth turf of the home park, where he and Old Ben had spent so many happy hours. He had been but five when Old Ben had left Stanton Manor, but he could remember the old man so plainly . . . so very plainly. It was a childhood memory and the more dear because of that. And now Old Ben was dead, killed by the plague. For years now he had assumed him dead, but the certain knowledge was nevertheless a shock, though the old man must have been a very great age.

"I thank you for coming," he said at last, viewing Ezekiel more kindly. "You shall eat and drink and be decently clothed. Tomorrow we will discuss the future."

Dr. Samuel Chubb watched the fellow shuffle out of the room. His eyes were speculative.

"I should not give my trust too easily, lad," he said.

CHAPTER II

In Which Ezekiel Hewitt Seeks Assistance

"I SHOULD question your new servant, Tom," said Dr. Chubb slowly. "Perchance he can throw some light on this affair."

Tom looked up sharply from his contemplation of books and papers strewn in disarray in his private closet. He had entered the room that morning to find every evidence that the house had been broken into during the night. The casement window swung wide, though the servant whose duty it was to bolt and bar the manor swore that the window had been fast locked by midnight, when Tom and his friend had retired to bed. The three chests in which the boy kept papers relating to the estate, account books, bills and receipts, had been forced open, and the contents flung haphazard about the chamber. Books from the shelves had been likewise treated, drawers torn from their niches and cupboard doors from their hinges. That robbers had entered Stanton Manor during the hours of darkness was beyond dispute.

Now, after two hours of enquiry, Dr. Samuel Chubb made his suggestion.

"Yea, I should speak with Ezekiel again," he repeated.

"I have already questioned the fellow," returned Tom shortly.

"But perchance he did not reveal all that he

knew," murmured the doctor. Then he put his hand on the boy's shoulder. "I told you last night not to give your trust too easily," he added.

Tom moved away, flushing angrily. From the moment that Ezekiel Hewitt had entered the library on the previous evening it had been evident that the doctor did not trust him; and in some strange way the knowledge fortified Tom's belief in the fellow. True he had been ill-clad and dirty, but that was no fault of his, but rather of the Navy Office, which had withheld the pay rightly due to him. After a wash and a regarbing the fellow had presented a very different appearance.

"I do not give a dog a bad name and hang him," said Tom. "The fellow took much pains to bring me Old Ben's message, and the least I can do is to repay him. He requires work, and since Robert fell ill I am in need of a servant."

His friend looked at him shrewdly for a moment and then shrugged his shoulders. He knew enough about youth to realize that even the most intelligent youngling will often be fortified in an action by opposition. The doctor had rarely seen a face which he mistrusted more than Ezekiel's. Within a few hours of the fellow entering the manor, a robbery occurred . . . and Tom stubbornly refused to admit that there was at least circumstantial evidence against the newcomer.

"So, you will have him as your personal servant?" he enquired. "Then we will not argue further, lad. Have your losses been heavy?"

"No . . . the thieves must have been disturbed, for no other room was entered. There was a bag of

B

twenty gold pieces, here, in this chest," pointing to one of the heavy wooden boxes, "and that has gone. Otherwise, nothing, I think."

"No papers, account books or records?"

"Not that I can trace. They would be no use to any but me." The boy paused, then swung round on his friend. "Sam, you do not trust Ezekiel?"

The doctor shrugged his shoulders again.

"I find it strange that you should have suffered this loss so quickly after his arrival."

"But . . . the window, Sam. The thieves entered from outside, for the window was swinging wide.

"An Ezekiel robbed you, lad, he would wish to give that impression. But . . . you have the right to employ the fellow if you wish."

Again the boy flushed, for his friend had made it very evident that he considered him a fool. Very well, let him so consider him.

"You must admit," he said suddenly, "that he speaks the truth when he says that he knew Old Ben. None that had not seen him could so describe his features."

The doctor nodded. There could be no doubt that Ezekiel Hewitt had known Old Ben, for on the previous evening, after he had washed and been provided with new garments, he had spoken at length of the old man, describing him so faithfully that even the doctor could not suspect him of lying.

"Yes, he knew Old Ben," he agreed, "but that does not prove him honest. But we will not quarrel, lad. Tomorrow we go to London."

They did not quarrel, but both were conscious of a tension between them. Tom was stubbornly determined not to be influenced by his friend's poor opinion of Ezekiel, and realizing that the doctor thought that he erred in his judgment and regarded him as a foolish youngling, became the more determined.

Old Ben he had never forgotten, for his kindness to a small boy roaming lonely through the great house, for his understanding and love. It had been a devastating shock when Old Ben had disappeared, and Tom could remember the consternation in the manor; the grief when it was decided that he must have been killed. The times had been troubled, with the country under an iron hand, with bands of licensed plunderers and murderers roaming the counties, pillaging and looting, especially in royalist counties such as Oxfordshire. Old Ben, an ardent royalist, had been in trouble with Cromwell's men before; it was only too likely, with the mock trial of Charles I then in progress in London, that he had lost his temper—and his life.

Old Ben, then, had not died at the hands of Cromwell's troopers. What, then, had happened to him? Why had he disappeared from Market Stanton on that night fifteen years ago? Where had he been living since, and why had he not communicated with his old friends? These were questions which Ezekiel could not answer, for he had come upon the old man but a short time before he was stricken by the plague, and only on his death bed, tortured by agony, had he spoken for the first time of Market Stanton. For Ezekiel's courage in remaining with the dying man in spite of the terrible risk of contagion, Tom was grateful.

No more was said on the subject either by Tom himself or Dr. Samuel Chubb, and on the next day, after making all arrangements for the well-being of the estate during his absence, the boy mounted his horse and with his friend rode away from Market Stanton, taking the road to London. Behind them rode Ezekiel Hewitt, a travelling trunk strapped to his saddle-bow. Tom himself had with him a smaller trunk containing his personal valuables.

As they reached the last point from which a view of Market Stanton and the manor could be obtained, the boy reined in and turned in the saddle to gaze at the house and village. It was strange to reflect that after so many years within the manor's walls and the confines of the village, he was now to leave it for many weeks; that in the morning he would awaken not in its familiar surrounding but in some strange chamber, attended by servants he had never seen before. Strange to realize that London, which he had seen but twice in his life, was to be his home for not less than two months.

"No regrets, Tom? Faith, lad, you are not leaving Stanton for ever! And London will be mightily good for you."

"Nay, I am not regretful," answered the boy, and then, "it is kind of you, Sam, and I am grateful."

The latter smiled, realizing that Tom was seeking to regain the old footing, which had been disturbed by the difference of opinion with regard to his new bodyservant.

"I am glad to have you," he said quietly, and thereafter they rode on peacefully, the doctor reflecting that England was as full of rogues as it

ever had been—perhaps more so—and that one
could not expect honesty amongst the lower orders
when it was conspicuous by its absence in the upper
classes. Corruption was rife, from the highest to the
lowest, in restoration England. The man Ezekiel
was no doubt a rascal, but perhaps no worse than
any other Tom might have employed. He was not
important enough to warrant the spoiling of a
friendship.

And so they rode on, through sleepy Oxfordshire, while the sun rose high in the heavens. The
roads were in good condition, for the weather had
been dry for many weeks, and though the dust rose in
clouds at the passing of any wheeled vehicle, the mud
which in the winter frequently reached to the hubs
of the coaches' wheels was mercifully absent. They
passed through Oxford itself—so lately the scene of
unwonted gaiety, for Charles had sought to
ameliorate his exile from London with masques and
fêtes, and took the London road.

The terrible plague, which had brought the life
of the capital to a standstill during the last year, had
not touched the country villages and towns, though
it had affected their trade and poverty was rife. But
these hamlets had not known the crunch of the death-
cart wheels, nor had the doors of the cottages borne
the dreaded red cross, the mark of death. Breathing
the sweet country air, Dr. Chubb wished that some
alchemy of science could take it to London, there
to bring sweetness and health to the fœtid mass of
crumbling, ancient buildings. It was only recently,
and as a result of continual outbreaks of plague that
men had begun to realize that overcrowding can

breed disease, and that narrow, twisting roads, so
narrow that those in the upper rooms of houses
could converse in whispers with friends in the
opposite houses, made it well-nigh impossible to
stamp out the epidemics. London was the greatest
city in the world; but it was also fœtid, overcrowded,
dirty and evil. Sometimes it reminded Dr. Chubb
of a great gross merchant, grown fat on his profits,
lazing away the days, too idle to wash or dress.

In the evening they came to a pleasant inn set
back from the road, and there they halted. On the
morrow they could reach London by midday, and
with the highways infested by cut-throats and
robbers, whose ranks were ever-swollen by unpaid,
discharged sailors who must rob or starve, and by
old soldiers of the troubled times of the civil wars,
who could find no other occupation in restoration
England, it would have been foolish to have pushed
on through the night. Only those escorted by heavily
armed men had any chance of crossing the heaths
near London and arriving safely at the capital.

The travellers swung from their horses in the
courtyard of the inn, left them in the charge of
ostlers, gave Ezekiel instructions to take the travelling trunks to the rooms they had bespoken, and then
entered the building, a place of low beams and
plastered walls. As they passed the door of a small
room the sound of upraised voices reached their ears.

"Damme, sir, I said no such thing! An you would
have the goodness to listen. . . ."

"Listen, say ye? Ha, I have better things to do
than to listen to the prating of—of a landlubber!"

At that there was a noise as of an explosion, and

upon flinging open the door, Sam and Tom were rewarded by the sight of Admiral Cocker apparently in the throes of an attack of apoplexy. Gripping the carved arms of his chair he was mouthing words which would not come, while his eyes near started from his head. A landlubber was he, by the saints? A landlubber! By those same saints, he would—he would . . . !

Dr. Chubb advanced quickly into the chamber, and laid a warning hand on the admiral's shoulder.

"'Twould seem I have come in time to bleed you," he said, smiling. "I have my implements with me."

The admiral glared, snorted—but subsided. His anger abated, and he fell to muttering imprecations.

"You amaze me, both of you," said the doctor. "What pleasure you obtain from this bickering is more than I can understand. Now, have done. You are returning to London, I take it?"

"We are, sir. I trust that you have no objection?"

Admiral Kenton was heavily sarcastic, and would no doubt have laboured the point if at this moment Ezekiel's face had not peered in at the door. The fellow, now that he was clean and soberly clad in good quality servant's apparel, was better-seeming than when the admiral had last seen him, but he was easily enough recognized.

"Ha, that rogue again," muttered Kenton. "Cocker, 'twould seem he cannot leave you."

Ezekiel, however, had swiftly departed before Cocker could turn his bulbous eyes to the doorway.

"What the devil are you talking of?" he demanded in a surly voice.

Tom broke in. Ezekiel had been in his services but two days, but it had already been proved that the fellow had not exaggerated his qualifications. He was quiet and apparently sober; and he was indeed able to cook and sew. He was, in fact, proving valuable, and the boy hoped that he was not about to learn something to his discredit.

"The fellow is in my service," he said. "Do you know him, sirs?"

"Only that he stated that he had served under Cocker," replied Kenton, "and Cocker recognized him—or said that he did."

"Said, sir, said? Do you imply I was lying, eh?"

Samuel made a helpless gesture.

"Come, Tom, let us leave our firebrands to their pleasure. 'Tis apparently our destiny to find them ever quarrelling. Perchance the plague will rid us of them!"

It was their destiny to be closely concerned with the admirals' affairs in the near future, and those affairs were to be of a nature so strange that had any warned Tom and his friend of how they were to be employed during the weeks that followed they would have been incredulous. But as they ate and drank in their private room, and later fell to talking of the plague, of the king, of his character and way of life, of the Dutch war which was going so badly, with the English fleet harried back to its ports, and finally of one Samuel Pepys, Clerk of the Acts at the Navy Office, it did not occur to them that they would have anything but the most casual acquaintance with the two admirals when they all reached London.

"Yes, Samuel Pepys . . . you must meet him,"

smiled Sam. "He is a man to be cultivated, lad. A strange person, bumptious to a degree, vain, fawning upon his betters and patronizing towards his inferiors . . . but an able administrator. They say, and I believe it to be true, that were it not for him we should have no navy. At court they laugh at him, but the king and the king's brother know his worth. He has worked hard for England. I will take you to see him. You have an ear for music, and that will commend itself to Samuel Pepys, who likes nothing better than to play the flageolet—unless it be to flirt with a pretty woman!"

"He sounds an unpleasant gentleman," answered Tom casually.

"Yes . . . but you must meet him. He calls me friend, and though it may sound strange to you, I value that friendship. He has some learning, and even now studies the records of the late troubles. Which reminds me, Tom. I took the liberty of passing on to him certain of your father's papers. I trust you do not mind? He will take great care of them, I can warrant."

Tom shrugged his shoulders. The papers were but rough records and memoirs of his father's experiences during the civil war, and were of no value except to the historian. Had it not been for Dr. Chubb's importuning, they would have lain dusty and neglected at Stanton Manor.

"I have no objection," he said. "And now, shall we seek our beds? We have a long ride before us tomorrow."

They had sat late talking, and it was past midnight when they settled down for the night. Three

chambers they had bespoken, a private parlour and
two bedchambers, for the doctor was a man of substance and always travelled luxuriously. In spite of
protests he insisted that Tom should be his guest
from the moment they left Market Stanton. The boy
would otherwise have journeyed in more spartan
fashion, but he found pleasure in the difference. For
the few minutes before sleep came he reflected
pleasantly on the weeks immediately ahead. He was
looking forward to his holiday in London.

Gradually the inn grew quiet as the last drinkers
sought their beds. By one o'clock the place was
silent. The pot-boys had gone to rest on their straw
pallets in dusty corners; mine host had made up his
accounts and was peacefully snoring in his four-
poster. Even in the private room shared by the two
admirals there was quiet, with Cocker dozing over
the cards, and Kenton yawning hugely. He had
drunk heavily, and his vision was slightly blurred,
so that the cards which lay scattered on the table
seemed to sway and merge. It was time to go to bed.
He staggered to his feet, picked up the gold coins
which were rightfully Cocker's, but which that
worthy would certainly not remember in the morning, and began to fumble with his jacket. It was then
that a noise from outside attracted his attention. He
paused, his ears strained. Somebody was moving
stealthily along the passage which ran outside the
chamber door.

Kenton moved to the door, weariness and a
fuddled head forgotten. Thieves, by the lord, for a
hundred guineas! Murderers, maybe, intent on the
cutting of throats as well as of purses. The admiral

was not drunk—it was doubtful whether, after a life-
time's toping, any liquor brewed by man could
render him drunk—but he was slightly fuddled and
possessed of the drinker's courage. As the stealthy
footsteps passed his door he flung it open, and with
drawn sword lurched into the passage.

All was dark except for the shaft of light which
spilled from the admiral's chamber, cutting a bright
swathe across the passage. In that shaft cowered a
man, who backed against the wall before the
menace of Kenton's sword. The admiral sur-
veyed him, and then stretching out a hand took him
by the collar.

"Ha, so you would cut throats, my friend! But
not tonight. What do you here?"

Ezekiel Hewitt's sharp little eyes darted hither
and thither, seeking a means of escape, but in vain.
The admiral was a heavy man, and in his hands
Ezekiel was helpless.

"I mean no harm, your honour," he gasped. "I
but come from my master's chamber."

The admiral grunted. Thomas Raynor's chamber, as he knew, lay but a few yards to the right. No
gleam of light showed under the door.

"You lie, you dog . . . unless you come with his
goods. What have we here?"

His sword was thrust back into its sheath, and
Kenton's free hand came out, to snatch a short
knife from the fellow's belt.

"And now, come you in here, and we will enquire
into this," said Kenton.

He jerked Ezekiel towards him and backed into
the room. Turning he swung the door shut behind

him, flinging the little man into the centre of the chamber, where he knocked into the dozing Cocker, thus abruptly waking that worthy.

"Eh . . . what? What the devil eh?"

Cocker staggered to his feet, glowering malevolently at Kenton and then in bewilderment at Ezekiel.

"Eh, what the devil?" he growled again. "Who are you, fellow, and what . . . 'death, you're the rogue who served under me. Were you aboard ship now, you'd have a hundred lashes for your pains, damme!"

Ezekiel retreated nervously, one eye on the door, which, however, was still guarded by Kenton. The latter briefly explained the circumstances, while Cocker muttered and presently poured more wine.

"Well, what have you to say, rogue?" demanded Kenton. "Who were you intending to rob, eh? You had better talk or . . ."

He did not complete the threat, nor was there any need to. Ezekiel cowered away, mumbling excuses. To these neither admiral lent an ear. Cocker, reaching forward, took the fellow by the collar and shook him like a rat, until every tooth in his head rattled.

"Now will you talk?"

Ezekiel groaned and rubbed his throat. His breath was coming in short, painful gasps. Then, as he somewhat regained composure, his little eyes sharpened, and his cunning brain, temporarily stultified by the sudden attack in the passage, began to work again. At last he spoke, and his words brought the advancing Cocker, who was intent on continuing the assault, to a sudden halt.

"What would you say, your honours, if I could tell you where to lay your hands on a king's ransom?"

There was silence. The remark was so utterly unexpected that neither Cocker nor Kenton could think of any adequate reply. Both were slightly fuddled, though action had cleared their brains to a certain extent, but there was that in the rogue's voice which carried conviction. Had he muttered some whining story to account for his prowling they would have known how to deal with him, but this talk of a king's ransom bewildered and nonplussed them.

It was Kenton who spoke first.

"What the devil do you mean?" he rasped—but already, as Ezekiel was quick to notice, there was an avaricious gleam in his bloodshot eyes. "What the devil do you mean?" he repeated.

Ezekiel, who had shown good judgment in believing that Cocker and Kenton would be interested in his story, passed his tongue over his lips. His throat was dry and still painful. He looked greedily at the wine on the table, and Cocker, interpreting the glance, thrust the bottle at him.

"Drink," he said, "and then talk, or you'll regret it."

Ezekiel grasped the bottle and drank. Then, wiping his mouth on the back of his hand, he spoke.

"Aye, a king's ransom," he said. "Silver and gold, plate, trinkets . . . that's what, gentlemen. But I need help. I'm only a poor man. You've got influence and you know how to manage such matters."

The two admirals glanced at each other. Both were thinking that it was possible that this rascal was speaking the truth, that by some strange chance he had information which would lead to wealth. In the late war much treasure had been hidden away, to save it from Cromwell's forces, or to await the king's need. Some had not been discovered, for those who had secreted it had died, and none knew its whereabouts. If this fellow had stumbled upon some cache, then. . . .

"Well, what do you know?" demanded Cocker. "And what has it to do with this prowling about passages after midnight?"

"I'm coming to that, your honour," whined Ezekiel. "Maybe you wondered why I came to Oxfordshire, and why I took service with Master Raynor? It was like this, your honours. . . ."

With few interruptions he talked for near half an hour, and when he had finished Cocker and Kenton were silent. The fellow's tale rang true. It was inconceivable that he had invented such a story on the spur of the moment. It was Kenton who finally spoke—soberly.

"If you speak truth," he said, "we will help you. If you lie, then you will regret it. Go to London with this Raynor, and keep your mouth shut. None must know that we assist you. None must know what you have told us tonight. And now get you gone, silently. You shall hear further from us."

Ezekiel nodded, moving to the door. He needed help, and he would have gone far to find better tools than Cocker and Kenton. Wealth in the form of plate and trinkets would be valueless in his hands, for to be in possession of such items would be to invite a charge of robbery. These two influential gentlemen, however, could transform the plate into gold coins. Though they were doubtless now planning how to convert the whole of the treasure to their own use, Ezekiel would take good care that he, and he alone, should gain possession of the money it would secure. One knife had they taken from him, but knives were common enough in London . . . knives with razor sharp edges. The thought of murder did not appal Ezekiel Hewitt.

CHAPTER III

In Which Tom Comes to Pudding Lane

LONDON was old, very old. That was Tom's pre-
dominant sensation as he rode through the capital
with Sam on his way to the doctor's house in Lombard Street. Old and decaying. Here was no proud
city of wide streets and broad squares, of white
walls and gracious palaces; but rather a mass of
huddled hovels, the plaster peeling from the laths
of the walls, the tiles hanging loose, the windows
broken, the roads mere narrow, winding lanes ankle-
deep in filth.

St. Paul's, its broken steeple rising above the
roofs which slanted in all directions, higgledy-
piggledy, dominated the city. From it the lanes
radiated, stinking, fœtid, alive with hawkers shouting their wares, with apprentices standing outside
their masters' shops raucously cajoling passers-by
to purchase, with jostling customers fingering the
goods on the open stalls, cursing, shouting, joking.
Alive . . . yes ! For all that its buildings were decaying, that last year it had been laid low by the terrible
plague, that only a few weeks had passed since the
Dutch had defeated the English fleet in the Four
Days' Battle and had since threatened the mouth
of the Thames itself, London was alive, with a
ruddy, boisterous life all its own. There was something about this ungainly, sprawling, dirty city;

something which gripped an Englishman and made him, unaccountably, proud of it. Heaven knew why Londoners should take pride in its dirt and grime and decay—but so it was, and if a foreigner dare condemn it, his life would not be worth a farthing. The true Londoner, stocky, thickset, possessed of a ribald humour—often macabre—was quick to revenge a slight.

When the news had come that the Dutch had defeated the English fleet and had appeared off the Thames, London had been dejected, and her citizens had inevitably raised the cry of treason. They had been sold to the French and the Dutch; Popery was at the root of their troubles. Some riots had broken out, but though the great lords and many of the wealthy merchants had sent their goods into the country, the capital had rallied to the shock. Men were ready to defend the city, and took up arms. Then, at the end of July, Monck and Rupert, going to sea with a refitted fleet, had secured a victory, sending the Dutch back to their ports. Now, in August, London sweltered but lived, noisily and gaily.

Tom, though a countryman possessing an instinctive distrust of all city ways, was conscious of an unreasoning pride as with Sam at his side he rode through the city, through the narrow, twisting streets where the houses nid-nodded to each other, and, in the alleys, merchants and customers were haggling and bartering. A great commercial centre was London, with its markets and shops jostling each other. There was the market at the Royal Exchange, where the grasshopper kept watch and ward. There was the Gracechurch Street market, selling herbs, sweet-smelling and medicinal, guaranteed to cure any ailment. At the Royal Exchange the stalls were stocked with every commodity, from gloves, ribbons, lace and hoods, to dolls, knick-knacks and toys. A decaying, dirty city—but the commercial centre of England.

At last Tom and his friend came to Lombard Street, where the wealthy merchants lived in their gilded, carved houses, richly designed, with great glass windows affording glimpses of luxurious chambers hung with gaily-coloured tapestries. Sam had deliberately ridden farther than necessary through the city, so that Tom might see something of the capital and its streets. What a vast difference, reflected the boy, between these gracious streets and the twisting alleys which clustered round the Thames, between St. Paul's and the Bridge!

As though reading his thoughts Dr. Chubb leaned towards him and spoke.

"It is a city of contrasts," he murmured, "as are all cities, though perchance London has more than others. But here we are, lad. You remember my house, of course?"

They reined in before a substantial house decorated lavishly in red and blue, the plaster cunningly worked into ornate designs. It was not so large as many residences in Lombard Street, but one glance was sufficient to prove that herein dwelt a man of substance, a man of taste. Glancing behind him for a moment Tom saw Ezekiel sitting his horse quietly a few steps away, staring at the house, his pleasure in discovering that he was to be so comfortably accommodated plain on his face. Ezekiel had comported himself most fittingly during the journey to London, and seemed to have his new master's well-being at heart. It was perhaps a pity that Tom, paying this slight heed to the doctor's words of warning, had refused to allow the fellow to sleep in the private parlour at the inn on the previous night. If he had not ordered him to seek a pallet in the servants' quarters, whoever had entered the bed-chamber would have been apprehended—or would not have reached so far. If anyone had, in fact, entered the bedchamber.

Tom shrugged his shoulders irritably. It was strange how it worried him to recall that sudden awakening in the pitch dark, to the consciousness that somebody was in his room. He had fumbled for box and tinder, had struck a spark only to reveal the chamber empty. He must have been dreaming—and yet in the morning he was sure that certain items had been handled and replaced in different positions. A chair, he was prepared to swear, was out of place; his private travelling-trunk was unlocked, whereas he had locked it before going to bed. Or . . . or had he perchance only intended to lock it? From being certain that somebody had entered the chamber he fell to doubting; and then again to being certain, and so continued, until he grew unreasonably irritated and attached more importance to the affair than it warranted. Nothing had been missing—and in any event, in roadside inns the traveller took his chance. Many cases of murder had been reported from such places. It was not unusual to be robbed while one slept.

For a little while Tom had wondered whether Ezekiel could have had any hand in the business. Since his coming one certain robbery had taken place, another was suspected. Sam had hinted . . . the boy set his jaw. His friend had warned him that this fellow might not be trustworthy, and he himself had refuted that suspicion. He was not going to alter his opinion. And . . . and he might well have been mistaken over the second incident Ezekiel's face was impassive as he gazed at the doctor's house, only in his eyes pleasure showing. With a sudden impulse Tom fumbled for a coin and handed it to him.

"You have served me well," he said.

Ezekiel took the coin and touched his forelock. The boy, conscious of Sam's sardonic gaze upon him, flushed a little and swung from the saddle. He knew himself well enough to realize that his pity for the under-dog sprang from a desire to make peace with himself. Ever since he could remember he had wondered that some men should be born into wealthy surroundings and others, through no fault of their own, to poverty and squalor.

Inside, the house was most comfortably furnished, with rich hangings on the walls, well-made furniture, delicate china and glass and expensive appointments. It was very spick and span, for Mrs. Knapp, the doctor's housekeeper, was an efficient woman and had a heavy hand held in much awe by the serving-wenches. The doctor's surgery was on the ground floor, a clean but simply furnished apartment, with new rushes always on the floor. Here Chubb and his partner Creid, a young man whom he had befriended and who in spite of bringing nothing to the partnership received a generous share of the profits, dispensed drugs and advice to those patients who could not afford the luxury of personal visits. As Tom well knew, Sam lost money in this surgery, for he could have made a great deal more by using all his time in visiting wealthy patients in their own homes. But Dr. Samuel Chubb was a strange man.

"I mulct the rich that the poor may benefit," he smiled, as later that day he took Tom to the surgery, where Creid was busy. "I charge exorbitant fees to such worthies as our friends, the admirals, and thus have time enough to do my real work." He paused and stared out of the window. Through the small latticed panes Tom could see a mother and child, the latter a girl of some eleven years. "You see that girl?" murmured Sam. "She was dying, and we saved her. One might almost say we saved her with Kenton's money—and Cocker's. They have wrought better than they know, they and others like them!"

His voice, which had lost its bantering tone for a few moments as he spoke of the child, was laughing again, his brown eyes as sardonic as ever.

"So, and yet you speak sometimes as though you doctors know nothing and can save nobody," said Tom.

"Ah . . . and it is true, isn't it Michael? We know nothing." He had turned to Michael Creid, a sallow-faced young man of some twenty-eight summers, in whose eyes plainly showed hero-worship when he looked at Dr. Chubb. Now he smiled but said nothing.

"What of the plague?" enquired Sam. "No cases, Michael?"

"Yes, there is one. In Pudding Lane. The place breeds disease like any dung-hill, sir. I wish . . ."

Chubb interrupted him, laughingly.

"Michael is ruthless, though perchance you would not think so from his appearance," he said, leaning his weight on his long, doctor's stick with the gold knob. "He would burn down all London, that Phœnix-like a new, clean city might arise from its ashes! A firebrand is our Michael!"

The sallow youth, plainly dressed in a buff coat laced with leather, and a white collar, bit his lip, and Tom saw that his hands were trembling. When he spoke his voice was high-pitched.

"Fire is the great cleanser," he said, "and this city is evil. It must be burned that its citizens may live. The plague, the rotting death . . . it will strike and strike and strike while we consent to this great dung-hill surviving." He paused for a moment, and Tom was conscious of a sudden tension in the air. Something . . . something indefinable but somehow frightening hung heavy in the atmosphere. Then, before either he or the doctor could speak, Michael Creid was talking again, and this time his voice rose to a frenzy and his eyes were wild. "The wicked city which hath spurned the Lord shall know the vengeance of the Almighty, yea, there shall be groaning and gnashing of teeth, and Babylon, that great city, shall be no more. Thus saith the Lord God."

He stopped suddenly. His face, which had become more pallid than ever, slowly took colour, flushed red. His eyes, which had stared, dropped.

His hands, still trembling, he thrust behind him.
There was silence in the surgery.

Then Samuel Chubb spoke.

"We must be going," he said quietly. "Tom,
can you amuse yourself until this evening? I have
much to do, but tonight I would have you meet Mr.
Pepys."

He turned and Tom followed him out of the
surgery. When they reached the doctor's private
closet, where his books and papers were housed, the
boy referred to the strange incident he had just
witnessed.

"Sam . . . I do not understand. Michael Creid,
he. . . ."

The doctor nodded, pursing his lips.

"He is a good doctor," he said, "and I have a
fondness for him. The sight of so many dead, of so
much horror, which none who were not in London
last summer can imagine, has set many men's minds
seeking for the cause. They believe that God has
struck at London for its wickedness—and who knows
that they may be right?"

"That may be, but your assistant is well-nigh
crazed, Sam."

Chubb shook his head. "No, Michael is not mad.
He worked night and day with scarce a pause during
the terrible summer of 1665, and his constitution has
been undermined. But he is not mad. Always a
religious man, he has turned even more towards
God as a result of the visitation of the previous
year.

"Such outbreaks are rare, Tom, and he is always
sorry afterwards, though there is no need to be. He

is harmless and as I have said, he is a good doctor. Do not worry, lad."

But the boy, as he wandered on foot through the city later that afternoon, filling in time until his friend should be at liberty, could not rid his mind of the thought of Michael Creid. Normal himself, he abhorred abnormality; and as a countryman he had no experience of the taut nerves of the city-dweller. To him it seemed incredible that Samuel could so airily dismiss the possibility that Michael was mad, for during those few moments of religious frenzy he had indeed seemed mad to Tom. But presumably the doctor knew what he was about.

Time did not hang heavily upon his hands as he walked through the city, for all was new and strange, and he surrendered himself to the teeming life of the streets. It was difficult to realize that twelve months ago this mass of streets had been near deserted, the shops and houses closed, the citizens keeping within doors, terrified of contagion. Now life was running swiftly through the narrow veins of the streets, and London, with the resilience which had always marked her and was to mark her for centuries to come, had recovered. Goods were once more pouring into her port, merchandise was entering the city by road from north, south, east and west. As Tom walked he was accosted by a multitude of voices, urging him to buy, to buy, to buy.

"Come, buy, sword-knots, gloves, silk stocks . . . come, buy my fine toys . . . come, buy, buy, buy!"

Tom pushed his way through the throngs, came to St. Paul's, turned down towards the river and so came to Pudding Lane. Here the way was even narrower, with the kennel full of dirt and muck, with the houses set at all angles as though they would fall at a push, with the paint and plaster peeling from them. A depressing street it was, running from Little Eastchepe to Thames Street near the Bridge, a street which unaccountably set Tom shuddering . . . until he remembered that here it was that there was a case of the plague. He pushed on quickly, noticed the red cross on one of the doors, averted his gaze and so approached Thames Street.

Now he felt better—and reviled himself for a coward. One case of plague and he had fled like a craven ! Yet Sam had stayed with death all around him, and Michael Creid, pallid and a physical weakling, with his thin, frail body and head too large and out of proportion, he, too, had remained.

Tom Raynor halted, and then retraced his steps, childishly and foolishly proving his manhood by walking back up Pudding Lane. He had walked some distance, and was approaching a baker's shop some ten doors from the junction with Thames Street, when out of a narrow doorway, set in a passageway between the baker's shop and the next-door house, lurched a man, an old man who mouthed and plucked at his loose lips. A tottering ancient he was, whose eyes had lost the light of reason, whose hair was in disarray and whose clothes were tattered and stained ; an old, old man, who must have fallen had not Tom grasped his arm. He helped him to stand upright, and then started back, an exclamation falling from his lips. This man . . . this old, mad man, was Old Ben ! Changed most woefully though he was, aged not only by the years but by the loss

of reason, Tom could not mistake him. It was Old
Ben beyond a shadow of doubt . . . Old Ben, not
dead. . . .

"Ben!" he cried, unheedful of the hurrying
throngs passing along Pudding Lane, and then
again, "Old Ben! Do you not know me? It is Tom,
Tom Raynor."

The old man mumbled unintelligibly, and then
his rheumy eyes fastened on the boy, and into them
flickered momentary recognition.

"Aye, Tom . . . little Tom. Will ye be riding
this afternoon, master? Or will ye have Old Ben go
walking with ye?"

He chuckled hoarsely, and then quite suddenly
recognition faded and he stared at Tom fearfully,
as at a stranger.

"Have done," he muttered. "Will ye assault an
old man?"

Weakly he pushed against Tom's chest, striving
to escape from the hand which still gripped his arm.
The boy felt sick at heart. Madness can appal and
revolt normality; now, for the second time in a few
hours, Tom was in contact with madness, and for
the second time he was revolted. In the case of
Michael Creid the madness had been but momentary, but it did not need a doctor to realize that Old
Ben was permanently mad. Quickly Tom subdued
his revulsion. This man had been his friend—in some
ways, servant though he had been, he had taken the
place of his father. It was not just that in his madness he should be spurned. Tom tightened his grasp
on the old man's arm.

"Nay, Ben, I am your friend. Do you not

remember? Little Tom was always your friend. You fought with my father at Naseby, and. . . ."

Old Ben, who had ceased attempting to escape, and stood slack, like a sack of flour, suddenly looked up. His eyes were bright.

"Aye, Naseby . . . Rupert's horse, we were with them . . . blood, I can see the blood. And the plate, master? Ye have the plate? Aye . . . 'tis safe enough. None but we two know. . ." He broke off and his face crumpled, like a child's when he has forgotten where he has hidden a favourite toy. "The plate . . . I have forgotten, master. I have forgotten."

Tom stared at him helplessly. Old Ben was mad, beyond all reason, pathetically unhinged. What was he to do with him? He should not be abroad like this, alone.

It was as he stood there still grasping the thin arm, that a voice smote his ears, an angry voice. A girl's voice.

"Leave him, sir! Have you no better mission than to assault a poor old man? Shame on you, sir!"

Even as she spoke, the girl sprang forward, tore at Tom's hand and thrust him aside. Then she turned swift to Old Ben, and her voice changed. She spoke softly, as to a child.

"There, there, do not fret, my dear. Jennifer is here. . . ."

Her arm went round Old Ben's waist, and she began to lead him away, back towards the doorway through which he had so recently stumbled. Over her shoulder she threw another angry word at Tom.

"Be off with you, and leave honest men to their affairs," she snapped.

The boy's face flamed at words and tone. To be accused of assaulting Old Ben was more than he could endure, and from a chit of some seventeen summers, whose copper hair was a glory, whose face, now sharp with anger, might well be beautiful in repose.

"It would be better, mistress," he replied coldly, "to enquire first and accuse afterwards. I was but helping this poor old man, who would have fallen but for me. Think you I would harm one who cared for me as a child?"

The girl stopped, swung round and stared at him. Her eyes, he noticed, were of a deep violet colour, the lashes long. Her mouth, no longer compressed in anger, was generous.

"He—he cared for you as a child, sir?" she repeated.

Tom bowed. The girl turned quickly to Old Ben, who was trying to move away, murmured soothing words to him, and then returned her attention to the boy.

"I am Thomas Raynor, at your service, mistress," he said. "Twenty years ago Old Ben rode with my father at Naseby field. He served my family faithfully and well. We thought him dead . . . and now I find him in London."

Little teeth came out to bite red lips. The girl flushed under Tom's straight gaze.

"I am sorry, sir, to have misjudged you," she said slowly. "But . . . but he is old and knows not what he does. Sometimes there is trouble. . . . Will you come with me, sir? My father will be glad to make your acquaintance."

Already a small group had gathered round them, eager for any sensation, and Tom nodded quickly. It was evident that Old Ben had fallen amongst friends; evident that the girl—Jennifer she had called herself—cared for the old man.

"I will come," he said, and followed her as she led Old Ben to the narrow doorway. In a few moments the crowd was shut out and Tom found himself in a simply furnished parlour, clean but by no means luxurious. Pudding Lane was not Lombard Street, and no wealthy merchants owned sumptuous houses so near to the Thames. Cheap shops, taverns, lodging-houses, these comprised the buildings of Pudding Lane, and Tom had no difficulty in deciding that William Tybald and his daughter lived by letting lodgings.

William Tybald, a lean, spare, grey man, with a lined, strong face, stood erect as Jennifer informed him of what had happened in the street and why she had asked Tom to come with her. He was clad in an old buff military jerkin, with leather laces, and was so obviously a soldier that the boy did not think to doubt this first impression. On the wall hung a long sword, providing corroborative evidence. Here, Tom decided, was one of Noll's old soldiers, eking out a precarious existence in a London now turned royalist. Not important enough, he and others like him, to hunt down and kill, as some had been hunted down, he was permitted to live—if he could. If not, then few would mourn his passing. The Raynors had been royalist, but Tom had heard enough tales of the prowess of Noll's Ironsides to feel some admiration for them. They had been godly

men, though their God had been hard and stern,
and they had fought with a discipline to which the
undisciplined English were not accustomed. Cromwell, for all that his bones had been dug up and
sacrilege committed upon his remains, had been a
great soldier; and his Ironsides had been invincible.

Tybald listened to what his daughter had to say,
and then bowed stiffly.

"You are welcome, sir. No doubt you will want
to ask us questions? Jennifer, my child, fetch wine,
and. . . ."

He gestured towards Old Ben, who was standing in a corner mumbling, and Jennifer went to him,
took him by the arm and led him away.

"I will fetch the wine, Father," she said.

As she went to the door she threw a swift glance
at Tom—and he felt his colour rise. She was, he
thought, about seventeen, not beautiful, and yet
there was a subtle attraction about her. Her features
had not the regularity of true beauty, but they were
alive, vivacious. Her body was slender and firmly-
knitted, as he could see, for her gown was simple
and not extravagantly cut, of a pale green which set
off her copper-gold hair. This was glorious, falling
naturally in waves to her shoulders. Her eyes, he
saw, were of a deep violet, though later he was to
discover that they changed often, from the deepest
shade to the lightest.

He was recalled to himself by Tybald, still
standing stiffly.

"If he were at Naseby, then perchance we have
met before," he said. "He was of the enemy?"

The phrase was hardly a question; it was more

of a definite statement. The man continued quickly,
defiantly.

"I fought with Noll," he said, "and now . . . but
I must not complain. I have not had the dogs of
London snarling round my bones as he has . . . and
Ireton."

Tom came forward. The troubled times were
past; he had no intention of seeking an argument
about a cause now forgotten. Forgotten? Nay
perhaps not forgotten, for while these old soldiers
of Cromwell's lived, it would be remembered.

"Old Ben has been with you long, sir?" he asked.
We thought him dead, first at the hands of . . . of
Cromwell's men, and then, later, of the plague. A
fellow brought me news that he had seen him
die."

He paused, remembering that Ezekiel had
indeed said as much—and therefore must have lied.
Yet he had described the old man perfectly, and
must have had some acquaintance with him. Here
was mystery.

Tybald did not answer the question, but waited
while Jennifer brought in the wine. This he poured,
offering a cup to his visitor.

"That will do, child," he said, and once more
she glided to the door, glanced at Tom and passed
through. Then the old soldier spoke to the boy.

"He came to us near three years ago," he said,
"and we knew not where he had come from. Only
his name did he recall, Old Ben. We have cared for
him since, for my daughter has fondness for him,
which has grown. It has not been easy . . ."

He broke off abruptly, but Tom realized that he

had been about to say that with money scarce it had not been easy to continue to feed Old Ben.

"I trust you will allow me to repay you," he said quickly. "He is more my responsibility than yours, sir. I will tell you how he came to leave us."

Rapidly he explained how Old Ben, safely returned from the wars, had left Stanton Manor on that fateful night, never to return; how it had been assumed that he had fallen foul of Cromwell's men, or possibly had been murdered by footpads, and how he had been thought dead.

"We could think no other," said the boy, "but not a week ago came one who told me that he had met Old Ben here in London, and had seen him dying of the plague."

William Tybald shook his head. By the mercy of God the pestilence had passed over his house. Old Ben had not been touched.

"What manner of man was this who brought you false news, sir? There was a man named Hewitt, a thin-faced fellow, who lodged here for a little. He talked much with Old Ben."

Tom's eyes widened. One mystery was solved, or partially solved; others were posed. Thus was explained how Ezekiel had been able to describe Old Ben, but it was not explained why he should have brought false tidings to Market Stanton.

"That was the man, sir. What know you of him?"

Tybald shrugged his shoulders. He knew nothing. The fellow had seemed to be a sailor, but that was the full extent of his host's knowledge. He had sought lodgings with the Tybalds, had stayed for three weeks, and had then left, whither none knew.

"And he spoke much with Old Ben?" asked Tom.

"Yes . . . there was some trouble. My daughter has almost a maternal interest in the old man," here Tybald's severe face broke into a smile, "and she did not care for the man Hewitt. We were glad when he went. You will already know that Jennifer is ever-watchful. This afternoon Old Ben escaped her vigilance, and she was worried, for if he leaves us we may never find him again, and perchance he will be thrown into Bedlam. That was why she was ungracious to you, sir, for which you have my apologies."

Tom waved them aside.

"What of Old Ben?" he asked. "At Market Stanton there is a home awaiting him, sir. And a welcome."

"Yes—yes, but he is . . . irresponsible, Mr. Raynor. And my daughter loves him. It is difficult. . . ."

Then he went to the door and called. In a few moments Jennifer and Old Ben appeared. The latter was calm by now, but his expression was vacant and he stared at Tom without recognition. The boy went to him.

"Old Ben," he said quietly. "Do you remember when you lived at Market Stanton? Do you remember John Raynor, and little Tom?"

The old man said nothing, did nothing, but stared blankly at the floor. The girl, Tom saw, was agitated, for one slim hand clenched. He realized that she suspected what it was he was about to suggest.

C

"Ben, will you come home with me?" he persisted. "Come back to Market Stanton, to those who love you?"

At that the girl suddenly flared up. Not for nothing had she been born with red hair.

"There are those here who love him, sir," she flashed, "aye, and have done much for him. Who are you to come here and . . ."

"Jennifer, have done," ordered her father. "You treat our guest discourteously. Would you have me beat you?"

The girl stopped, turned white and began to weep. She turned and moved to the door, disregarding Tom's attempt to halt her. He was left embarrassed and unhappy. He had known her less than half an hour, had exchanged but a few sentences with her, yet he was strangely moved to see her in tears.

As she left the room Old Ben began to mumble, and then to cry. It was pathetic to see the tears coursing down his wrinkled cheeks. As Tom knew, he was at least eighty years old, yet he looked more, looked incredibly ancient as he crouched by the wall weeping. Tybald, recognizing the signs of a coming outburst, moved quickly forward, but he was too late. Without warning Old Ben slid to the ground, writhed for a few moments and then lay still. William Tybald raised him in his arms and laid him on a simple day-bed which stood in the room.

"This has happened before, sir," he said. "I think there is no cause for alarm."

He opened the door and called, and at once the girl came. She was no longer in tears, but she gave

Tom not a glance as she entered the room. Swiftly she went to Old Ben and ministered to him, while the two men stood by and watched. After a few minutes the old man recovered consciousness. He stared at the girl, then at Tom, and began to mutter. His hand clutched Jennifer's arm.

"Don't let them take me ... let me stay with you."

"Of course you shall stay," said the girl softly. "Of course you shall stay."

She shot a defiant glance at Tom, who nodded.

"He shall stay," he whispered. "I but strove to relieve you and your father of the responsibility which is rightly mine."

She neither accepted nor rejected this plea, but turned away, back to the old man. He was muttering again, though his eyes were closed.

"The gold," he whispered, "the gold ... the king's gold. We hid it. There was plate and gold ... to hire men. They mustn't find it, master ... they'll not find it, only you and me ... we know. Make the plan, lest we be killed ... make the plan, master. Look, they are holding ... by all the saints, they are holding! Rupert comes ... the pikemen are holding ... nay they have broken, they have broken. ..."

His voice rose to a crescendo, and as he crouched there listening to the ravings of this man who had been like a second father to him, Tom Raynor could almost hear the clash of swords, smell the stench of gunpowder, see the lines of charging men as Rupert of the Rhine led the great charge at Naseby field. Old Ben was back again, fighting, cursing, swearing ... back again on that fateful field fought in

June, 1645. On the day-bed he writhed and twisted, shouted and cried aloud with pain.

And the three who watched were silent in that little room, two men and a girl. One of the men had fought at Naseby with Cromwell; the girl was his daughter; the other man was the son of a royalist who had fallen on that field. It was a strange and dreadful scene, poignant, heart-rending. Tom's face was strained as he listened and watched. How had old Ben come to this woeful pass? What dreadful things had happened to him during the years since he had left Market Stanton, years which might more mercifully have brought him death instead of the bodily strength which so often is the gift of lunacy? Had it been destiny which had led his feet to Pudding Lane this afternoon? The boy shivered. He felt as though in a net, a net woven by some mysterious power which held him in thrall.

It was late in the afternoon before Old Ben fell into a coma and then passed into a peaceful sleep. Late before Thomas Raynor left the Tybalds' house and sought Lombard Street once more.

CHAPTER IV

In Which There is Uproar in Seething Lane

Dr. Chubb wrinkled his forehead, while one hand gently stroked the small moustache which he wore in honour of Charles II.

"So, he remains in Pudding Lane?" he murmured. "'Tis an extraordinary tale, Tom. Old Ben, twice dead, yet not dead at all!"

The boy, returned to Lombard Street in the early evening, and now sitting with his friend in the private closet, nodded.

"Yes, he remains there, Sam. He is out of his wits and thought that I would harm him. And the girl . . . she has a fondness for him and I would not . . . offend her. I have paid Tybald money for his keep."

Chubb pursed his lips. His eyes were smiling.

"Ah, the girl. She was lovely, this daughter of an old rebel who bore arms against the king?"

"No, not lovely, yet . . . what is loveliness, Sam, but in the eye of the beholder? And the man, he bore arms, that is true, but it was long ago. He will remain in peace for all that I shall do to bring him down."

Samuel Chubb smiled more broadly. So, beauty was but in the eye of the beholder? A very true statement, but not one which he had expected from a boy new fallen in love. And Tom, he surmised, had indeed fallen in love, though perchance he was not yet prepared to admit it even to himself. His defence of the man Tybald was no less than Sam had expected.

"He remains in peace," he agreed. "The king has other matters to attend to besides hunting down the poor tools of Cromwell and Ireton. But what of Old Ben, lad? You would like me to see him?"

Tom was eager for this. Sam was a doctor, and perchance could say whether there was any hope of the old man's regaining his senses.

"Yes . . . but I warn you, lad, there is little chance. He is old, near eighty, and at that age . . . but we will see. What of the last twenty years? Have you no information of his life? Did he not babble of those years in his ravings?"

"No . . . only of old fights, of Naseby certainly, I think, and of treasure. I have told you."

He glanced sidelong at his friend, but Sam remained silent, staring at the table before him, frowning in thought. Tom, too, relapsed into silence.

"Perchance he fell in with Cromwell's men," he said at last, "as we believed, and received injuries which drove him mad."

"That is possible, probable, even, for lack of other evidence. But who can tell? The human mind is a strange and delicate instrument, Tom. It is but balanced on the razor edge of reason, and often enough it fails to keep that balance . . . and though there must be a cause, rarely can we find that cause. There are other matters of even more importance to discuss. What of Ezekiel's tale now?"

"It would seem, Sam, that you were right ... and that I was wrong," muttered Tom. "I trusted too easily."

"You are young, and the young always trust too easily. You have to live many years in this woeful world to discover that truth and honesty are rare virtues," smiled the doctor. "But enough of moralizing. It matters not whether I was right and you wrong. I judged the fellow to be a rascal, but had no idea what particular roguery he planned. Now, perchance, we may hazard a guess.

"Ezekiel lied," continued Sam slowly, "but we may believe that he knew Old Ben. On that point we have the evidence of the Tybalds and need not doubt it. The fellow comes to Market Stanton and gains your favour by his tale of Old Ben's death-bed ... and within a matter of hours your papers are searched. Later, on our way to London, your room was once again entered."

"You think, then, that robbery was not the motive?" muttered Tom.

"Nay, I think robbery was the motive, lad, but that the rascal was seeking not gold—though he could not resist the temptation to steal that which lay to his hand—but . . . your father's papers."

Tom leaned forward eagerly. Now were they approaching the crux of the matter. There could be but the one motive for such robbery; and Dr. Samuel Chubb must realize that.

"You mean, Sam, that my father hid plate and gold before Naseby fight, and left directions of its whereabouts in his papers?"

The doctor rose to his feet and went to the window. For some moments he stared out into Lombard Street, silently. Then he turned, and there was a whimsical smile on his handsome face.

"It is odd that I should believe such a thing," he said, "but . . . yes, I do believe it. I have but dipped into your father's papers, but from them I learned that before Naseby fight he was in command of Bury Manor. You remember . . . but no, perhaps you were too young. The place was burned to the ground by the rebels after the battle."

"Yes . . . ?"

Samuel Chubb leaned forward, hands on the oak table. He was no longer smiling.

"As I said, I have but glanced at the papers—but I remember this. Your father noted that at Bury Manor was housed part of the plate and gold brought in by loyal squires to the support of their king. *And your father was in charge of this wealth and responsible for its safekeeping.*"

There was a long silence when he had finished. Tom's brain was working rapidly. Old Ben had babbled of treasure, of secreting it, of the fact that only he and John Raynor had known of its whereabouts. Ezekiel Hewitt had known Old Ben for a short time, and had often talked with him. He had then made his way to Market Stanton, had gained employment with the Raynors—and had searched Tom's private papers. Once again, probably, failing to find what he sought at Stanton, he had searched at the inn. He must have believed that amongst John Raynor's papers were directions for finding the wealth secreted before Naseby fight—and Tom judged that Ezekiel was not the man to act blindly. Old Ben must have referred to such papers; amongst which might be certain documents which the old man himself had brought back from Naseby, saying nothing of their contents for fear that the enemy would seize the treasure. Old Ben had disappeared long before the Restoration, while Cromwell was still in power. Tom himself had been but a child, too young for Old Ben to confide in; his mother was not the woman to feel any interest. Thus Old Ben would certainly have kept his own counsel, waiting until the king came into his own before disclosing the whereabouts of the hidden wealth. The theory was plausible.

"Then . . . we have but to search the papers," said Tom. "Ezekiel has not discovered them, for you have them here, Sam. Unless . . ."

"No, he has not discovered them here," replied the doctor, "for I have lent them to Mr. Pepys, as I told you. Perhaps you have forgot? But do not fret. We shall meet Mr. Pepys this very night, as I warned you."

"What of Ezekiel?" demanded Tom. "I was a fool, Sam, not to trust to your judgment of the fellow. We have a score to settle with him."

"Yes, but there need be no haste, Tom. The papers are safe enough. There is another matter . . . we are but surmising, though I think our surmises are correct. But we may be wrong, lad. Old Ben may have raved, or the treasure may have been discovered long since, or there may be no papers. 'Tis certain, I think, that we have made no mistake in believing that Ezekiel is confident that papers and treasure exist, but we have no proof that he does not err. Do not expect too much."

Tom nodded—but in his heart he was not convinced by his friend's argument. Treasure . . . buried treasure! Gold and plate, brought in by the country squires and landowners for the support of the martyred Charles I! Treasure lying hid for all these years; lying still beneath the blackened ruins of Bury Manor, near Naseby! The boy's blood thrilled at the thought. He had no wish to believe it untrue. His family was impoverished, the estate was in need of money to restore it to its one-time splendour. If this treasure could be found, then. . . .

"It is the king's property, Tom," murmured the doctor, breaking into his thoughts. Then, seeing the boy's face drop, "but I have no doubt that his Majesty will be generous to those who assist him to his own. Come, lad, we will away to Mr. Pepys' house. Had I known what those papers might contain, they would not have left my possession. But Mr. Pepys is a careful man, and I have no doubt they are safe with him." He paused, and then added, "you will find other interest in this meeting, lad. Penn and Batten will both be present, and perchance we shall discover whether our late victory over the Dutch has indeed prevented invasion."

Tom, however, was not overmuch concerned even with such an important matter. Sir William Penn and Sir William Batten, the first a Commissioner for the Navy, and the second Surveyor, were no doubt authorities on England's present disastrous naval situation—for the victory of July 25th had by no means eliminated the Dutch threat—and Samuel

Pepys, now Surveyor-General as well as Clerk of the Acts, and responsible for the victualling of the fleet, was as certainly cognizant of the condition of the navy, but Tom was far more interested in the possibility that in his father's papers were instructions for the discovery of the treasure secreted on the night before Naseby field. Like all Englishmen he was apt to underrate any danger from outside, and instinctively to assume that in the long run all would be well. The Dutch, after their victory in the Four Days' Battle at the beginning of June, and their subsequent threat to the English coast and the Thames itself, had been driven back.

Of Ezekiel Hewitt there was no sign when the two left Lombard Street and made their way to Seething Lane, wherein was situated the Navy Office and the residences of the principal officers, including Pepys, Batten and Penn. None in the Lombard Street house knew where Hewitt was, but this mattered little; he could be dealt with later.

"We will have a few words with the rascal when we return," said Dr. Chubb. Then he laughed, remembering a certain treasure hunt in which Samuel Pepys had been implicated—and which had ended in complete failure. "Perchance for a time we will say nothing to Mr. Pepys on the subject," he murmured, "for he might not take it kindly. I doubt if he has forgotten his search at the Tower!"

In 1662 an informer had come with word that £7000 was buried beneath the Tower, this money having been secreted by one of the republican governors during Cromwell's administration. Lord Sandwich had enlisted Pepys' help, and the latter had flung himself into the hunt with typical enthusiasm. The result had been complete failure to discover the treasure, and Mr. Pepys had felt a fool—which he did not relish. It was likely, therefore, that he would not wish to be drawn into another abortive search.

"I had no intention of speaking to Mr. Pepys on the subject," replied Tom. "When we have found the papers, then must we discuss what measures to take."

His friend nodded. It would indeed be necessary to decide their next move carefully. Any wealth which might yet lie hid at Bury Manor would be his Majesty's property. An attempt to discover it without royal authority might be disastrous.

"Yes, we must step warily," he said, " and Mr. Pepys could assist us. There are many matters to be considered, lad. His Majesty will not wish, I think, to have the matter made public. Let the Commons hear of this and the king will receive little of the wealth. But we will talk of it later—if need be. As for Mr. Pepys, an we could persuade his good offices . . . but that, too, is for later discussion."

By now they had arrived at the house in Seething Lane wherein the Clerk of the Acts resided. It was not large, but upon it Pepys had lavished money, and it was pleasant enough, looking across the courtyard of the Navy Office, so that the Clerk of the Acts was always within easy reach of his work. This had both advantages and disadvantages. The visitors entered and were taken immediately to the parlour on the first floor, where they found the company assembled. Tom could not but feel interest at this first sight of Samuel Pepys, for the doctor was not the man to give his admiration easily, and the fact that he did admire this full-faced, consequential man, was in Tom's eyes substantial evidence that the Clerk of the Acts had ability.

As he bowed ceremoniously, the boy cast a keen gaze upon his host. He saw a man of thirty-three, plump and round of face. The nose was large, the mouth full, and the eyes were luminous and almost woman-like. He was well dressed, with finely embroidered waistcoat, expensive lace and ruffles, and a coat of gaudy hue, well cut but a trifle exaggerated. He held himself with conscious dignity.

"I bid you welcome, sir," he said. "Lord, how hot it is! And you, doctor, welcome to my poor house. The company you know, I think?"

The reference to his house was made in such a way that Tom realized that it was not intended to be interpreted literally. And he decided that whatever ability this man might have, he did not like him. There was both an arrogance and a humility apparent—and Tom judged that Samuel Pepys was a man who would be arrogant with his inferiors and humble before his betters.

"Yes, I am acquainted with Sir William Penn, and with Batten," murmured the doctor. "And with your wife. I give you good evening, Mistress Elizabeth."

Mrs. Pepys curtsied and made herself pleasant. She was a pretty woman, some seven years younger than her husband, and was not less attractive by reason of her slightly French accent, which she had inherited from her French father. Her conversation was by no means intellectual, and to put no fine point on it, she babbled—and it was noticeable that her husband showed some irritation, glancing at her angrily from time to time.

Dr. Chubb smiled. He knew the Pepys family well enough to realize that their married life was peculiar. For the most part Samuel was the master; but on occasions Elizabeth could show her mettle, and then poor Samuel would wilt before her fiery temper. Chubb sometimes wondered whether Mrs. Pepys obtained pleasure from appearing to be afraid of him—and he would have given much to be present during the periodical quarrels which the neighbours said took place.

"Ah, we have our firebrands with us, too," murmured the doctor, his eyes resting on Admiral Kenton and Admiral Cocker, who were drinking in a corner. "We must speak with them, Tom."

The boy, however, was not interested in the two admirals.

"What of the papers?" he murmured.

His friend laid a hand on his arm. Mr. Pepys had the papers, and there was no cause to press for their return.

"We will wait a little longer," he said softly. "We must not appear to be anxious, and 'twould seem discourteous to mention them yet. Before we leave we will request their return."

He motioned Tom forward, and approached the little group of people who were standing near the open window sampling Mr. Pepys' wine. It was dark by now, for Chubb and Tom had not left Lombard Street until the evening was well advanced;

a cool night breeze, welcome after the heat of the August day, was coming through the window. Sir William Penn was speaking, emphatically. He was a round-faced man, fair-haired and in his way attractive, very different from his colleague Sir William Batten, who was squat, tub-shaped and usually unpleasant, being dictatorial both in his cups and out.

"The whole conduct of the fight," he was saying, "was ill. Two-thirds of the captains were against the battle, but were afraid of being called cowards. They should have waited for Rupert to come up. When they fought it was without discipline, sir!"

Sir William Batten, who invariably argued whether he agreed or not, merely for the sake of arguing, broke in angrily.

"Nonsense, sir. They fought bravely, as Englishmen should."

The doctor turned to Tom, his mouth close to the boy's ear.

"They speak of the Four Days' Battle," he said, "at the beginning of June. They have argued on its tactics ever since." Then, to Batten, "Yes, sir, bravely though they fought, they were defeated, and the Dutch paraded before our coasts. Were it not for Monck and Rupert proving victorious but a few days since, we had like to have Dutchmen marching through London."

At that the argument became more general. Kenton and Cocker, representatives of the old school of sailor, which had it that a captain must fight his ship to the death and nothing more, supported Batten in his contention that during the disastrous Four Days' Battle, all that could have been done had been done. Chubb lent his support to Penn, who maintained that captains must fight in line, instead of promiscuously, and that vessels must not return to port to refit during the course of the battle. It was a heated argument, the men growing angry, the women—apart from Elizabeth Pepys there were two or three other ladies—watching, frightened that a brawl would occur. There were in the room four admirals—and it was therefore not surprising that tempers rose and voices became loud and hectoring! None of the admirals was an easy man to live with in peace, and none liked to be contradicted.

Samuel Pepys remained silent for the most part, though Tom saw his lips moving from time to time as though he would have liked to interrupt but dare not. At last, however, he did speak.

"Lord, what nonsense is this?" he demanded. "The Dutch have been driven back, God be praised, and can we but find the men for the fleet so will they remain. I would to God that we need not press men for service, for they make but poor sailors, and their families are much distressed. 'Tis a great tyranny, sirs."

Kenton spluttered with rage at this opinion. A great tyranny, by the Lord? What other method was there by which men could be secured for the fleet?

"Chicken-hearted, by the plague!" he exploded.

Samuel Pepys paled a little, but would have stood his ground had not Elizabeth come forward.

"Enough," she said. "Samuel, let us have music."

Her husband glanced at her angry face, and then—to Chubb's inward amusement—made haste to obey her.

"Aye, we will have music," he said. "I have this day secured . . ."

He did not complete his sentence, for at that moment uproar broke out from another part of the house. Voices were raised, and to the guests' ears came clearly the cry, 'Thief! Stop thief!' This was followed by a woman's screams.

Silence descended on the parlour, but only for a moment. Then there was a rush to the door, while the three ladies raised their voices in excited questions, and Elizabeth Pepys grasped her husband's arm.

"'Tis thieves again!" she shrieked, "Samuel, I 'ave warned you . . . mon Dieu, 'ow I 'ave warned you!"

In this excitement she reverted more than ever to a French accent. Mr. Pepys dragged at her arm.

"Silence, wench," he ordered, and then broke off as a serving-boy came into the room, struggling through the men who were jostling in the narrow doorway.

"Well, what is to do?" shouted Pepys, in a sweat —as he put it himself later—for the safety of his precious goods.

"Thieves, master . . . in the closet. Quick, and we may have them yet. Will holds one rogue fast!"

CHAPTER V

In Which a Pursuit Takes Place

As Tom ran up the stairs which led to the second floor of the house in Seething Lane, edging past the rest of the party and in some cases forcing his way to the front, a question was clamouring for answer in his brain. Sam had given the papers to Mr. Pepys, and that information Ezekiel Hewitt might well have come upon, either by eavesdropping during the journey to the capital, or by some other means since arriving in London. Was it possible that it was he who was responsible for this burglary in Seething Lane? That he had come not to rob Mr. Pepys of his goods, but of John Raynor's papers? Was it Ezekiel Hewitt who was even now being held in the closet on the second floor?

The male guests swept up the narrow stairs, jostling and pushing and shouting. Kenton and Cocker, Tom had time to notice, were not in the van, and he assumed that they considered discretion the better part of valour. In this, however, he wronged them —though at that time he had no idea why they had no strong desire to reach Mr. Pepys' closet quickly. He himself, throwing courtesy to the winds, forced his way to the front, thrust both Pepys himself and Sir William Penn aside as they reached the landing, and thus came into the closet first.

He had one glimpse of two men struggling in the

middle of the small chamber, and of a woman, her apron over her head, whimpering in a corner. Then one of the men gasped and fell away, his hand to his side, while the others, still holding the short knife which had already drawn blood, sprang for the window, a small casement of leaded panes hanging wide. Tom was after him without hesitation. Pepys' servant was evidently wounded, for blood was flowing from the wound in his side, but there were others able to assist him. Tom, young and lithe, went after the man whom he had recognized instantly as Ezekiel Hewitt.

The closet was on the second floor, but only eight feet below the window a roof sloped down nearly to the courtyard which separated the house from the Navy Office. The quarry hung from the window-sill for a moment and then dropped to the roof. He slithered down the tiles and was lost to view in the darkness as he leaped from the lowest part of the roof to the ground. Tom was halfway through the window as Pepys, Penn and Chubb reached the wounded man. They called to him but he had no time to reply. Following Ezekiel's example he dropped to the roof; lost his footing as he landed, rolled to the lower edge, and unable to save himself fell heavily to the ground. Fortunately the drop was but five feet or so, and though bruised and shaken, he was uninjured. In the excitement almost unaware of his bruises, he scrambled to his feet.

From the other side of the courtyard came the noise of running footsteps, and Tom was after the quarry on the instant. From the window above him came shouts, and glancing back briefly he could see

Pepys himself thrusting his head through the open casement, behind him the vague figures of others. Then he was across the courtyard and out into Seething Lane.

Here all was in darkness, except for a few lighted windows, but the quarry could still be heard ahead. Tom followed, and proof that he had made no mistake was forthcoming when Ezekiel passed swiftly through the shaft of light coming from a suddenly opened door.

With a sudden thrill Tom then realized that the fellow did not know that he was being followed. This was proved by the fact that after a few moments his pace decreased and he fell into a quick walk, being evidently unwilling to attract attention by continuing to run.

The figure ahead was now walking more slowly, and without warning came to a sudden halt. Tom began to close up, stealthily. He was within ten yards of Hewitt when the latter moved again, vanishing into the darkness. Tom reached the spot where he had been standing, dimly illuminated by the light from a nearby window, and found that here Seething Lane ended abruptly, debouching into a road which ran east and west. He hesitated, his ears strained, but not a sound of footsteps reached him. Ezekiel Hewitt had been swallowed up as though he had never existed. Tom was angry with himself. He should have raised the hue and cry, called upon the watch or any of the householders whose windows had been lit as he passed, not have relied upon his own single-handed efforts. Ezekiel might have turned either right or left along the cross road—there was no indication which route he had taken.

Tom turned to the right, advanced a few paces and listened again. No sound reached him. He retraced his footsteps to the corner of Seething Lane, this time turning west. Was that the sound of footsteps, borne on the night breeze? He listened again . . . yes, somebody was moving ahead of him, but it might well be some innocent traveller. Ezekiel had been given some minutes in which to make good his escape. Tom reached a sudden decision and pushed on to the west.

The road ended in another, running north and south. Tom's knowledge of London was small, but he thought that this street was Mark Lane—and was subsequently proved correct. With nothing to go on, for the footsteps he had heard had now ceased, he turned north, once again towards Fenchurch Street. From a large house some two hundred yards up Mark Lane, lights streamed. With a sudden quickening of his breathing, Tom saw a cloaked figure pass one of the windows and turn into an alley which edged one side of the house. Abandoning all precautions he ran forward, found the mouth of the alley and plunged down it. It was pitch dark, but as he entered the alley a door suddenly opened, a shaft of light spilled out, striking the opposite wall, the passage between the large house and its neighbour being narrow, and a cloaked man passed through. As he did so he turned his head slightly, revealing the features of Ezekiel Hewitt.

For a few moments Tom hesitated. He knew where his quarry was, but how to smoke him out? He went

to the narrow door which opened into the alley, and
his hand was raised to knock when he realized that
little good could come from such an action. Ezekiel
must have been either expected or else had a key to the
door. In either event it was certain that he was known
in the house. It was beyond the bounds of possibility
that he had feloniously entered the building, for
there had been nothing furtive in the manner in
which he had entered. It was possible that those in
the house had no knowledge that he had so recently
broken into Mr. Pepys' residence at the Navy Office,
but Tom realized that his own tale of following the
man through the darkened streets would sound
implausible, and that any accusation might well be
laughed at.

The house was large, and must be owned by a
man of some wealth. Ezekiel Hewitt, who had
entered by a side-door, was no doubt unknown to
the owner, and was probably friendly with one or
other of the servants. Tom could imagine the result
if he sought an interview with the owner, told his
tale, answered questions, persuaded the gentleman
who had probably never heard of Ezekiel Hewitt,
that he was not a madman, and finally succeeded in
having Ezekiel sought. By that time the fellow
would have made his escape once more, and Thomas
Raynor would be accused of foolishness, if no worse.

Slowly he walked back along the alley, into
Mark Lane and so came to the front of the house. It
was a well-kept residence, timbered and gabled,
with plaster heads of angels on either side of the
main door. Undoubtedly it was the property of a man
of wealth—a merchant, perchance, or . . . Tom

moved quickly back into the shadows, away from the light spilled from the windows, as a coach lumbered over the cobbles and drew up outside the house. Two gentlemen alighted, and as they did so Tom's eyes widened.

"Think you that he has come?" said one, as he stepped from the coach.

"Enough," snapped the other. "We will talk when we are within our own walls."

He approached the door and thundered upon it with the hilt of his sword. The other followed him, and when the door was flung open by a servant, both men passed inside, leaving Tom to his astonishment. So. Ezekiel Hewitt, returned from robbing the house in Seething Lane, had come straight to Mark Lane—to the residence of Admiral Kenton and Admiral Cocker! It was inconceivable that either could have any knowledge of the fellow's activities . . . and yet, could it be mere coincidence? Was it but luck that Ezekiel had an acquaintance with a servant in this house of all others in London?

Tom remained motionless in the shadows long after the coach had departed. Cocker, upon alighting, had enquired whether his companion thought that somebody, unidentified had yet arrived. Ezekiel Hewitt had arrived but a few minutes earlier. Moreover, the fellow had some acquaintance with Cocker, having served under him. Both admirals had been at Market Stanton when Ezekiel had reached that village; they had been at the inn when Tom and Sam had arrived on their way to London.

Upon an impulse the boy approached the door

and knocked. With the servant who opened it he was commanding. He must see Admiral Kenton and Admiral Cocker without delay, upon urgent business. The servant eyed him askance, for his tumble from the roof in Seething Lane had dirtied his garments, and both hands and face were soiled. But Tom insisted, and eventually the servant took his name and would have gone ahead to announce him had not Tom followed hard at his heels and thus come into a small, oak-panelled room to find not only the two admirals there but Ezekiel Hewitt as well.

"Devil take me, what ... ?"

Kenton sprang to his feet as the door opened and the servant entered. Then his eyes fell on the boy, and he was silent. That he was greatly embarrassed was evident. Cocker also rose to his feet, and stared at Tom owlishly, completely off his guard.

It was Kenton who recovered his wits first.

"I bid you welcome, sir," he said. "Plague on it, what brings you here? The last I saw of you was as you vanished through the window! Did you lay hands on the rascal?"

"I did not lay hands on him," returned Tom, "but ... I saw him clearly enough. I followed him to this house."

"You .. you what, sir?"

It was Cocker's turn to speak. His little eyes went swiftly first to Kenton and then to Ezekiel. The latter's face was impassive, but Kenton's was suffused, either with anger or fear—or both.

"I followed him here," repeated Tom, "but I recognized him in Mr. Pepys' closet, and thus it matters not whether I followed him or not. He is here now and you may see him with your own eyes, sir."

There was silence, broken at last by Ezekiel himself.

"I have been here for some hours, sir," he said quietly, "and can prove it. Rumbold has not left me, sir," he added, turning to Cocker.

"Rumbold, eh? A trustworthy man. What have you to say, Mr. Raynor?"

Cocker was regaining his composure, and now stared at the boy aggressively.

"There were two thieves, I believe, though I saw but one. Perchance . . ."

"Nonsense, sir! Plague on it, would you turn my servants into thieves, eh? Rumbold has been with me, aye, and with Cocker, these ten years." Then, tugging at a bellrope he bade the servant who answered it fetch the man Rumbold.

"And there is Clewitt, your honour. He was with us," whined Ezekiel, his little eyes fast on Tom's face as he spoke.

Half an hour later Tom left the house in Mark Lane, and returned to the Navy Office. The man Rumbold, a thick-set fellow whose manner and bearing proclaimed him as an ex-sailor, had vouched for the fact that Ezekiel Hewitt had been with him all the evening, and that neither had stirred abroad. Clewitt, who was evidently loyal to both Rumbold and his two masters, had corroborated this. Yet Tom knew that Ezekiel had been at Seething Lane, that he had robbed Mr. Pepys' house and had come straight to Mark Lane. A conspiracy was afoot, and it was not difficult to guess its purpose.

He reached Seething Lane to find the house still in an uproar, though many of the guests had now left, and others were leaving. As Tom arrived Sir William Penn was taking his leave, and his colleague Batten followed on his heels.

"Well, Tom, what of your adventures?" demanded Dr. Chubb, grasping him by the arm.

Before he could reply Mr. Pepys had come up, excited and voluble.

"Lord, what a pother there has been," he exclaimed, "but the Lord be praised, nothing of value stolen. What of you, Mr. Raynor? Did you lay hands on the rogue? My man swears there were two, and the boy has multiplied the number by ten, but 'tis my opinion there was but one."

"I did not lay hands on him," replied Tom shortly, and glanced at his friend as he spoke. He did not wish to answer a multitude of questions.

Samuel Chubb interpreted the glance correctly, and turned to Pepys.

"The streets are abominably dark," he said, "and no doubt Mr. Raynor occupied himself pursuing shadows." And then, addressing Tom once more, "The loss Mr. Pepys has sustained," he murmured, "concerns you, Tom. A packet of your father's papers, which Mr. Pepys borrowed, have been stolen by the rascal. 'Tis unlikely that they can be of any value," he added meaningly.

Tom nodded. So, Hewitt had been successful in securing the papers. It was not politic, however, to inform Mr. Pepys of their true value.

"I regret that you have suffered loss," said

Pepys, "and 'twas not charitable to think only of my own good fortune. Gad, sir, but I forget my manners!"

He continued in this vein for some moments, condemning himself for his shortcomings in not preserving the papers in better safety, reviling the lawlessness of the times, and abjectly apologizing for the mishap. Yet it was evident to the boy that he was overjoyed that none of his own possessions had been stolen.

"No doubt the rascal would have pilfered your plate had he been given the opportunity," murmured Dr. Chubb, "but was disturbed before he had done aught but rifle the chest where you kept the papers. But we must be away, sir. Little harm has been done. Come, Tom."

They left Seething Lane without more ado, and returned directly to Lombard Street. It was not until they were alone in the doctor's private closet that the subject of the papers was again mentioned, for though Tom had attempted to speak of his adventures in darkened London, Chubb had prevented him.

"Wait, lad, till we are safe from eavesdroppers," he had said.

Now, at last, he turned to the boy.

"Well, Tom, what happened? You spoke but half the truth when Mr. Pepys enquired?"

"Yes. I did not lay hands on Hewitt, but I saw him plain enough."

"Ah, so 'twas Hewitt in Mr. Pepys' closet? Continue, Tom. You followed him?"

The boy nodded, and briefly recounted his

adventures between leaving Seething Lane by way of the roof, and returning thither. Dr. Chubb listened without interrupting, but his interest was evidenced by his eyes, bright and shrewd, fastened on the boy's face.

"There can be no doubt," ended Tom, " that Kenton and Cocker are aware of what really happened, and condone the theft of the papers. We shall not see Ezekiel again," he added, "he remains as servant in Mark Lane."

"So . . . he remains as servant." Chubb rose to his feet and carefully poured wine. "It would seem, then, that our firebrands may now be in possession of information which may or may not lead them to wealth secreted by your father before Naseby field, Tom. We must assume, I think, that the rascal Hewitt succeeded in gaining possession of all the papers—Mr. Pepys informs me that this is so—and that they do contain the necessary directions."

He paused, tapping his slender fingers against the wine glass, so that it rang musically.

"'Tis possible, even probable, that no wealth will be found, either at Bury Manor or elsewhere," he continued slowly. "But we cannot presume that. Well, Tom, what next?"

The boy gripped the hilt of his sword. Chubb was right—there might be no treasure, but until this was proved, for his part he intended to assume that there was, and that the admirals now had possession of the instructions which would lead them to it.

"They shall not beat me so easily," he said grimly. "The papers must be recovered. They are my property, and if found in the possession of either

Kenton or Cocker, they shall answer for it to the law."

Dr. Samuel Chubb smiled. Tom Rayner was out of touch with reality.

"Kenton and Cocker," he said, "have his Majesty's confidence. You will not find it easy either to prove unlawful possession or to secure their punishment. There is, perchance, another way. Old Ben is still alive, though witless. Already he has, in his babblings, told you something of value. He may tell you more. Tomorrow we will visit Pudding Lane, Tom, and do what we may to unlock his tongue. He knows where the wealth was hidden. Let us discover its whereabouts, and I trow we shall reach Bury Manor before the firebrands!"

Tom was silent. A robbery had taken place, his property had been filched; that property was now in the possession of Kenton and Cocker, he had no doubt—and yet he himself, the lawful owner of the papers, must seek to discover what those documents contained by going to Old Ben. Was there no justice in England?

"The rogues should be hanged," he growled.

"Perchance, though we should lose much amusement," returned Sam. "But what would you? You cannot force your way into their house, Tom, and think you that to lay an information against them, personal friends of his Majesty's, would bring you any reward? What proof have you that Ezekiel Hewitt robbed Mr. Pepys? None but the witness of your eyes. What evidence that any papers which he may have stolen are now in the possession of either Kenton or Cocker? None whatever. You must be

guided by me, lad. If Old Ben fails us, then must
we reconsider. Until then, put away all thought of
making this thing public."

Tom drank his wine moodily. Sam, of course,
was right; but it went against the grain to permit the
two admirals to beat him so easily. Yet there was
nothing else to do.

"Very well," he growled. And then, "Sam, think
you that the papers in truth contain directions?
Think you that treasure still lies at Bury Manor or
nearby?"

Samuel Chubb clapped his hand on the boy's
shoulder.

"What do I think, Tom? I do not think . . . I but
hope. But I must say this. The fact that the rogue
Hewitt believes that this wealth may still exist, and
that our friends Kenton and Cocker are persuaded
of the truth of it, does not prove its truth. But we can
hope!"

Thus they separated and sought their beds. The
next morning they made their way early to Pudding
Lane, and as they approached the house next door
to the baker's shop, Tom was conscious of a great
desire to hurry. And this desire he knew, though he
was loath to admit it, was not entirely due to the
possibility that Old Ben might be persuaded to talk
again of the treasure hidden twenty years ago.
Jennifer Tybald would probably be at home . . . and
Tom had not forgotten her strange attractiveness.

As they passed the house upon which was
scrawled the red cross warning passers-by that the
plague had struck, the doctor indicated it with his
stick.

"Michael attends," he said briefly, "and . . . but here he is."

The door had opened, and Michael Creid had come out. He paused to exchange a few words with the watchman on duty outside the infected house, and then turned in the direction of Thames Street. When Chubb hailed him he turned with a start.

"Well, Michael, and what of your case?" enquired Samuel. "All goes well?"

The young man's pallid face twisted as though in pain. He seemed unwilling to talk of the plague case.

"I . . . I cannot tell," he muttered at last. "'Tis too early to be certain."

The other doctor glanced at him sharply.

"You follow the usual treatment?" he enquired.

Dr. Creid's eyes dropped. The thought crossed Tom's mind that he was afraid, though it was impossible to discover any reason for fear. Certainly it was not of the plague, for the young man had already proved his courage in the previous year.

"I have made up poultices," muttered Michael at last. "Yolk of egg, turpentine, London treacle . . . I should like to bleed her."

Sam shook his head. He was prepared to admit that the treatment usually given was not efficacious, and that those who recovered from the disease were probably not affected by it, either favourably or unfavourably. But he was averse to experimenting on patients. The plague had abated; he did not desire his patients to die as a result of a search after new treatment.

"No, Michael, do not bleed her. I have told you before."

The other said nothing, but turned away. Once again Tom was conscious of something abnormal about him, something almost frightening. It was as though within him was some force, some evil force which peeped out occasionally through his pale eyes a force kept but uneasily within bounds.

The three walked in silence down Pudding Lane, and stopped outside the Tybalds' house.

"We visit here," said Sam. "I give you good day Michael. We seek an old, witless man. Perchance you have some knowledge of him? He has lived here for some three years they say."

Tom was standing a few paces away, waiting for Michael Creid to go. He had a strange feeling that he did not wish the young man to see Jennifer, or the girl to see Creid. It was foolish, but the girl was so fresh, so sweet, and Dr. Michael Creid, for all his youth, was as though of another world, a decaying world of disease and death. A huge man evidently the baker himself, was standing in the doorway of the shop which stood next to the Tybalds house, arms akimbo, watching the group. Idly Tom glanced at him, noting the great arms and legs, the moon-like face, the small mouth and bright blue eyes.

Before Michael could reply, the man moved forward.

"He's gone," he said, jerking one huge hand in the direction of the Tybalds' house. "Went early this morning, God rest his soul."

Michael, who evidently knew the man, frowned

"He is dead?" he asked. And then, turning to Sam, "He speaks of Old Ben, of whom you were enquiring. This is Master Faryner, who bakes bread for half the City."

"Aye, and for his Majesty himself," interpolated the baker. "Best wheaten bread, sirs, for the court." Then, reverting to Old Ben, "Took at four o' the clock this morning, and a happy release, for he was mad and should by rights have been in Bedlam. You must go to your betrothed, doctor," he added, with a sly wink. "She'll be needing your consolation, for she was mighty fond of the old man."

"Yes . . . yes, I must to her," muttered Michael Creid. "I . . . you are coming in, sir?" he asked, turning to Chubb.

The latter nodded, and moving to Tom's side, put his hand on the boy's arm.

"I did not know," he murmured. "Michael is somewhat secretive. But come, lad, wear not your heart upon your sleeve."

Tom pulled himself together. Michael Creid, betrothed to Jennifer Tybald! It was incredible . . . and yet, why should it not be so? London was a large city, but Michael's professional duty brought him to Pudding Lane, and Old Ben had no doubt been in need of his attentions during the last three years. Such a match, between his daughter and this clever young doctor, William Tybald would no doubt consider greatly to his advantage, as a one-time supporter of Cromwell now forced to eke out a precarious existence. There was little to wonder at that it had been arranged.

But as he thought of Jennifer Tybald and Dr.

D

Michael Creid as man and wife, as he remembered her sweetness and unspoiled youth, he shuddered. Such a mating was a crime, but who was he to pass judgment? What right had he, who had seen the girl but once, had spoken with her for but a few moments, to interfere?

As he followed his friend into the house he knew by what right he felt thus. His was the most ancient right in the world—the right of the man who has fallen in love with a maid.

CHAPTER VI

In Which Tom Raynor Knows both Hope and Despair

TOM gazed down on Old Ben, lying in the silence of death on the narrow bed. The boy had looked only twice before on a dead man, and on each occasion it had not been a pleasant sight, for each had died suddenly. But there was nothing frightening about Old Ben as he lay so quiet. Death had been kind to him, kinder than life during the years of his madness. The lids of the eyes were closed, so that the eyes themselves were hidden; strangely the years had dropped away, and the face upon which Tom now looked was that which he remembered as a child—and there was no sign of insanity. Old Ben had gone to his rest, and Tom could not feel unhappy for him. Death for the old man was better than a witless life.

He stayed for some minutes gazing at the man who had been so kind to him. He was remembering past scenes, past experiences. At last Chubb touched his arm.

"Let us go," he said quietly, and Tom rose to his feet. He felt a reluctance to descend to the parlour, where Jennifer and Michael might well be in occupation, but he could not remain in this narrow room, and eventually he must see the girl again. It was better to do so at once.

As he followed his friend down the steep staircase, his thoughts returned to Market Stanton.
There was a girl, Margaret, the daughter of Sir
John Walker, whom once he had thought to love.
He had known her since childhood, but . . . long ago
he had realized that he could not marry her. He had
decided that women were not for him, and that
though his duty might be to continue his line, yet the
Raynor family must be allowed to die out rather
than that he should take any woman to be his wife.
And now . . . he scarcely knew Jennifer Tybald,
and yet he loved her, knew that he must wed her or
for all his life be but half alive.

At the foot of the stairs Dr. Chubb paused. "Old
Ben cannot help us," he said. And then, "but the
king may be able to."

With an effort Tom tore his thoughts away from
the girl.

"The king?" he repeated.

"Yes, his Majesty is a poor man, and is ever
eager to lay his hands on wealth. This treasure, if it
indeed exists, is his property. We might do worse,
Tom, than lay the facts before him. And Mr. Pepys
can help us, lad. His Majesty looks upon him with
some favour. What say you? Shall we trust Mr.
Pepys with our confidence? I can vouch for his
honesty."

The discovery that Michael Creid was betrothed
to Jennifer had temporarily destroyed Tom's
interest in the strange affair of the Bury Manor
treasure, and now he agreed without demur to Sam's
suggestion.

"Take Mr. Pepys into your confidence an you wish it," he said.

Dr. Chubb glanced at him sharply, but made no further comment. Instead he opened the door of the parlour and stood aside for Tom to enter.

Four people were in the room, Tybald and Faryner, talking together near the door, and the two young people sitting on the window-seat. As Tom entered his eyes went swiftly to the girl. She was clad in the same green gown which she had worn on the previous day; the sunlight, streaming through the latticed window, fell on her copper hair and made it glint. Her eyes were dark and shadowed.

She rose to her feet as Tom and the doctor came in, and Michael followed suit after a moment, though his eyes remained on Jennifer and he did not spare a glance at the newcomers. There was a blind worship on his face which Tom was quick to see.

"You have . . . you have seen him?" enquired the girl, her face pale, as Tom could see now that she had turned slightly towards the window. One hand was at her breast.

"Yes. I have taken my leave of him," he replied quietly. "I am sorry, mistress. You were fond of him and his going must be a sad loss to you."

She was silent for a moment, her eyes on his face. Then swiftly she dropped them, but not before a slow colour had mounted her cheeks.

"I . . . I thank you, sir," she said.

That was all, but Tom's heart was beating quickly. Was he verily a fool to imagine that she had risen to her feet so quickly to avoid an unwanted

contact with Dr. Michael Creid? Was it sheer
foolish fancy that, though perchance unwittingly,
she had flashed a message to him now? That . . .
that she found him more interesting than her
betrothed? It seemed foolish indeed, and yet . . .
still there was colour in her cheeks, and her bosom
was rising and falling more rapidly, as though she
were agitated.

"You have my gratitude," he said at last, "you
and your father, for all that you have done for my
old friend. I am indeed grateful."

William Tybald broke off his muttered conversation with Faryner the baker.

"We were glad to be of assistance, sir," he said.
And then, to his daughter, "Jennifer, I would have
you oblige Mr. Faryner. There is bread to be taken
to Mark Lane, and I would have you deliver it.
Mr. Faryner is busy and . . ."

The baker broke in at this point. Aye, he was
busy indeed. Never had there been such a demand
for his bread, and that rogue of an apprentice of his
was ill again.

"Plague on it, he is never well!" exploded
Faryner, with a grimace, "and if their honours do
not receive my bread there will be a fine to-do, that
I promise you."

It was Dr. Chubb, hitherto silent, who now spoke.

"My friends Kenton and Cocker reside in Mark
Lane," he murmured. "Do you bake for them,
Master Faryner?"

"Aye, that I do indeed, sir. They pay me well for
fine wheaten bread such as you cannot procure elsewhere in this city. 'Tis firebrands they are, begging

your honour's pardon if they are friends of yours, and much abuse do I have to endure, but they reward me well, and I am a poor man. Poor indeed since the king. . . ."

He broke off as Tybald interrupted him swiftly.

"My daughter will take the bread," he said. "Get you ready, mistress, and do not delay."

She went to the door, and Michael Creid followed her.

"I will escort you, my pretty," he said, the endearment sounding strange from those pallid lips. "The city is no place for a God-fearing maid, even in broad daylight. Sin and evil are abroad, even in the king's palaces."

William Tybald made a sudden movement as though to interrupt, but Chubb was before him.

"You have an urgent case in Thames Street, Michael," he said softly. "Would it not be as well to attend to that duty? Mr. Raynor and I return to Lombard Street, and will most willingly escort Mistress Tybald."

Michael stared at him sullenly. His pale eyes passed from the doctor to Tom, whose face was impassive though the blood was racing through his veins at the possibility that he would be permitted to accompany the girl to Mark Lane. For a moment it seemed that Michael would defy his partner, but Jennifer spoke swiftly and curtly.

"To your duty, Michael," she said. "I do not need you."

The young man bit his lip, and then without a word picked up his hat and stick and went to the door. Still silent he passed through. William Tybald addressed his daughter.

"That is no way to speak to your betrothed," he said. "I have told you before that . . ." He hesitated, and then, evidently unwilling to enter into an argument with others present, gestured to her to begone. "Get you ready," he said coldly. "We will speak of other matters later."

Jennifer withdrew, and for a few moments there was an uncomfortable silence in the parlour. Tom's eyes were upon the ground, his thoughts busy. Jennifer had no liking for her betrothed, of that there could now be no doubt; it was also certain that her father greatly desired the match. Idly the boy fingered the hilt of his sword. Little grounds for hope had he, for how could a maid of seventeen go against her father's wishes? And yet much more hope had he now than when he first entered the room. Jennifer was not uninterested in him, he was sure of that—and she had spirit. Tom had seen and noted the look she had flashed at Tybald as she left the room.

"Young love knows not its own mind," laughed the huge Faryner suddenly, breaking the silence. "Let them but be wedded, and we shall see whether lad or maid will be the master! I remember . . ."

"Enough," said Tybald harshly, and as Faryner relapsed into a somewhat shamefaced silence, swiftly turned the conversation, speaking of other matters, of Old Ben and of Tom's assurance that he would pay the expenses of the funeral. As he spoke, Tom's eyes were on him. Though his mind was full of Jennifer, though her very presence had served to push away all other matters, yet he was conscious of a strain, of a tenseness in the small chamber, and he groped for an explanation.

Twice Tybald had seemed agitated, once when Faryner had evidently been about to make some derogatory remark about the king; again when Michael Creid had spoken of the sinfulness of the city ... of evil being abroad even in the king's palaces. Yes, again the king had been mentioned. Tybald was an old soldier of the Commonwealth, and thus might wish to avoid any suspicion that he himself criticized his Majesty. That was plausible enough, and yet, though there was not an atom of proof, the boy felt certain that there was something else, something more important behind his manner. He glanced at him again. William Tybald was standing straight as a pike, his arms folded; his face was cold and severe, the eyes without emotion. But stay, were the eyes indeed impassive? Lurking behind them was a hint of suppressed feeling ... the man was wrapped in thought, and those thoughts, Tom was confident, were not pleasant. And what of this connection with Kenton and Cocker? Was it merely that Tybald's friend baked bread for the two admirals? Or was there some other, more sinister connection? Had this anything to do with the strangely tense atmosphere?

Angrily the boy thrust these vague theories and suspicions from him. He must be losing his wits. Tybald had been a supporter of Cromwell; there was every reason why he should not wish his friends to air critical views before comparative strangers. As for his thoughts, they were his own and no man could guess their purport. They might deal with a hundred different matters. As for there being a strained atmosphere, that must be sheer imagination.

His own thoughts were interrupted by the return of the girl, and within a very short time all three were walking up Pudding Lane on their way to the wealthier district of Lombard Street and Mark Lane. Jennifer's gown reached the ground, but she caught it up over one arm so that the fabric should not trail in the filthy street, revealing a glimpse of green stockings and high-heeled shoes.

As they came to the corner of Gracechurch Street, neither Tom nor Jennifer having as yet spoken a word to each other, Samuel Chubb keeping the conversation alive, the latter halted.

"I must crave your pardon, mistress," he said, "and you, Tom. I have an appointment which I would not break. Mr. Raynor will escort you safely to Mark Lane, mistress. I give you both good day. I will see you anon, Tom."

He smiled at the two young people, his brown, handsome face almost puckish, and then turned away, leaving them alone together. Tom gazed after him, grateful for what he knew to have been a gesture of good will, but now that he had Jennifer to himself he was ill at ease, as tongue-tied as any yokel. It was with an effort that he turned and looked at the girl—to find her smiling at him.

"That was kind of your friend," she said quietly, and though spoken by another the words might well have sounded brazen, in her mouth they were but the natural expression of her thoughts. Then, realizing what she had said, she flushed shyly.

Tom could scarcely believe his good fortune.

"Yes, it was kind of him," he said. "You, too, think that, mistress? Or were you but being courteous?"

The girl would not look at him, but at last she spoke.

"I meant it," she said.

He took her arm, and slowly they walked up Gracechurch Street, lingering at the herb market, both making the most of these few minutes together. They spoke of trivialities, unwilling to touch on more important matters, until Tom abruptly dropped the mask as Jennifer was examining one of the stalls.

"My sweet," he said quietly. "What of Dr. Creid?"

She turned, and he could see that her eyes were shadowed. She, too, came into the open.

"He is my betrothed," she said, "and my father greatly desires the match. 'Tis understandable, for we are poor, and now, with ... with my father's cause lost, our life is not easy."

He nodded. It was indeed understandable that William Tybald should seek security for his only child. But what of her? What of the girl who was to become Michael Creid's wife?

"I . . . I dream of it o' nights," she answered, "and Tom, I . . . I think I hate him. He frightens me. When he touches me I . . ."

There were tears in her eyes, and for a wild moment he was tempted to take her in his arms, for all that Gracechurch Street was thronged.

"Then you shall not wed him, my sweet," he said. There was silence while she recovered her composure. When at last she spoke again it was as though tears had never touched her eyes. Her voice was steady.

"Come," she said, "people gape at us."

He glanced round, flushed angrily at the interested stares of the passers-by, and then taking her arm walked on. After a few moments he spoke in her ear.

"Sweetheart, I have known you but twenty-four hours, short enough a time in all conscience, and yet . . . long enough."

She did not attempt to pretend that she did not understand him.

"Yes, long enough," she answered, and for a brief moment looked him in the eyes.

Then, Tom carrying the basket of bread, they walked on again, through the seething, milling crowds which thronged the herb market. Her arm was under his, and looking down at the copper-gold hair which came but to his shoulder, Tom found it well-nigh incredible that she could have come to mean so much to him in so short a time. And so they came to Mark Lane, to the house occupied by Kenton and Cocker, and there parted.

"I have come here before, on behalf . . . on behalf of Master Faryner," she said, the hesitation barely noticeable. "They will provide me with an escort home." And then, as Tom made to speak, "No, Tom, do not wait for me. It will be better if you do not return to Pudding Lane with me."

"But Jennifer, I must see you again. When may I . . ."

"Soon, perchance," she said, and turning, left

him solitary. Once she waved, and then was gone, turning down the narrow alley at the side of the house. In a few moments the side-door through which he had watched Ezekiel pass on the previous night was opened and she had gone.

It was some hours later that Tom, in company with Dr. Chubb, sought Mr. Samuel Pepys at the latter's house in Seething Lane. Forcing himself to take renewed interest in the subject which, until the discovery that Michael Creid was betrothed to Jennifer, had absorbed all his thoughts, Tom explained to the Clerk of the Acts the exact course of the strange affair of the Bury Manor treasure— if indeed treasure still lay hid in that locality. Samuel Chubb remained for the most part silent, but Pepys himself was constantly interrupting the recital, with excited questions, half-completed comments, and exclamations of astonishment and often of incredulity. The perky little man was apparently unable to remain still for more than a few moments at a time, but paced the floor of his private chamber in Seething Lane, fiddled with his flageolet, which was always at hand, and generally behaved not unlike an excitable child. When at last Tom ended his story he burst into speech.

"Plague on it, lad, 'tis beyond all belief! 'Tis a monstrous tale! Lord, that I should . . . yet, perchance 'tis not so monstrous. Gad, doctor," wheeling round on the amused Chubb, "Gad, it might have some foundation in fact!"

The doctor was not surprised at the manner in which Pepys veered from incredulity to optimism. The man was volatile, impulsive. Those who did not know him well thought him a fool; Chubb did not accept this judgment. Samuel Pepys had his foibles, as had all men—perchance he had more than most —but for all that he was shrewd enough.

"Yet, it might have some foundation," murmured Chubb. "Who can tell? Nobody . . . until the matter is put to the test. As I conceive it, we lose nothing by so doing."

Pepys pursed his lips. Nothing to lose? Chubb was right, up to a point. Neither the doctor nor the lad Raynor had anything to lose . . . but what of Mr. Pepys? He had his reputation to lose. There had been that unhappy business at the Tower, about which his Majesty had not yet ceased to laugh. And yet, if there was any truth in this tale, it would be mighty pleasant for the Clerk of the Acts to have a hand in bringing it to a successful conclusion. Kenton and Cocker evidently believed in the story; and the rogue Ezekiel. Yes, there might be something in it.

Chubb was speaking again, chin on the gold knob of his stick.

"We come to ask you, sir, to approach his Majesty," he said. "We have no influence at court, but you . . ." He shrugged his shoulders, and Pepys visibly preened himself. It was a constant source of joy to him to know that the king himself, and his brother the Duke of York, treated him familiarly. "The papers have been purloined," continued the doctor, "and though we know who now has them, we cannot retrieve them. His Majesty, however, will be able to exert influence in the right quarters. Kenton and Cocker will find it politic, I think, to return them to us when they realize that the king is aware of the facts. We hope that you, Mr. Pepys, can assist us in this matter."

Pepys pulled at his lower lip. He had the king's ear, certainly, but suppose that this was but a mare's nest? On the other hand, if it should prove true . . .

"Very well, I will speak to his Majesty," he said, making up his mind. "Perchance he will wish to speak with you. Hold yourselves in readiness."

He then proceeded, with much enjoyment, to instruct them in court etiquette, which they suffered without complaint, for it was amusing to watch Mr. Pepys preening himself upon his knowledge of such matters. Then once more they fell to discussing the possibility of plate and gold lying in Northamptonshire, and eventually left the Clerk of the Acts to solitary meditation, making their way back to Lombard Street.

Pepys, for his part, was still torn between two desires—the desire to have a hand in this affair if it should prove successful, and an ardent wish not to be implicated if it should prove a mare's nest. Not for the first time in his life the little man wished he could have his cake and eat it! His romantic nature triumphed, however, and the next day he was determined to seek out his Majesty and retail the extraordinary tale of him. With care it could be arranged that if nothing came of it Samuel Pepys could appear only to have passed on some idle chatter as an amusing anecdote; whereas if treasure were discovered, then the Clerk of the Acts could be made to seem a vital factor in the business.

In the meantime Tom and Chubb reached the

Lombard Street house in friendly silence. There was nothing fresh to say about the treasure; all had been said. The admirals had the papers, and thus probably knew the whereabouts of the treasure. Tom, the rightful owner of the documents, and his friends, were ignorant of where it lay. Thus, until such time as the papers were returned, nothing further could be done. As they reached the doctor's house, the boy spoke.

"I pray you to excuse me, Sam," he said. "I have . . . a matter of some urgency to attend to."

Sam looked at him smilingly. He could hazard a guess what that business was—and that it would take the boy to Pudding Lane.

"Then fare you well," he said. "But Tom, have a care. There are those who would not wish you well an they knew what was in your heart."

The boy stared at his friend for a moment, and then abruptly took his leave.

When he reached Pudding Lane the darkness had closed in, though it was not yet pitch black and he could see the houses on the other side of the street. William Tybald's house was in darkness when he arrived, but even as he drew level with it a window in the front was illuminated. Tom saw a shadow thrown across the window—a girl's shadow. Then, even as he gazed, furtive footsteps sounded behind him, and involuntarily he shrank against the wall. A man passed him, reached the Tybald's door and knocked three times. The door was immediately opened and he passed through. Before Tom had time to leave the shelter of the wall another figure passed him, cloaked, with the hat pulled down over the eyes. Again three quiet knocks could be heard, and again the door was opened.

The boy came away from the wall. There was a narrow passage between the house and the baker's shop next door. Tom stepped into it, glancing round at shadowy walls, trying to gain his bearings. As he did so other footsteps sounded in Pudding Lane. He grew tense, waiting and listening. Yes, the footsteps had stopped at the Tybalds' house. He was too far away by now to hear any knocking, but a shaft of light spilled into the street for a moment as the door was opened. Quickly it was closed again.

Tom frowned. Who were these men who had come to Pudding Lane so furtively? What reason could have brought them to the house of William Tybald?

His thoughts were interrupted dramatically. In the darkness, greater in the passage than in Pudding Lane itself, he had not been able to see that he was standing by a narrow door which opened from the house into the passage. This was suddenly opened and a figure emerged, carrying a lanthorn. By its dim light Tom could see Jennifer Tybald, the hood of her cloak drawn over her head.

As she stepped into the passage she knocked into him, and drew back with a startled exclamation. He was quick to reassure her.

"It is I, sweetheart, be not alarmed. It is Tom, Tom Raynor."

There was silence, broken only by the sound of her quick breathing. Tom had the sudden impression that she was at bay, like a trapped animal. Then she raised the lanthorn so that the light fell on his face.

"Yes, 'tis you," she muttered. And then, her tone changed sharply. "What do you here? What right have you to peer and pry, sir? Begone, before I call the watch."

It was as though she had slapped him across the cheek, the attack was so sudden, so startling.

"But sweetheart, Jennifer, I . . ."

"Get you gone, sir," she said harshly. "Get you gone. I desire no conversation with you."

It was not only the words she used, but the tone of her voice which brought the blood to Tom's face, and set his heart beating unevenly. Into her voice she had crowded dislike, anger and it seemed to him utter loathing.

Turning, he stumbled into Pudding Lane, and like a man bemused walked away from the little house next to Faryner's, the baker's.

CHAPTER VII

In Which the King Speaks, and Tom Returns to Mark Lane

HIS MAJESTY King Charles II possessed an unusual charm of manner, of which Tom became instantly aware as he entered the quiet gallery in the palace of Whitehall and beheld the king awaiting him.

Impossible as it is to define charm, those who knew Charles well—though it is open to doubt whether any knew him really well—were at odds when attempting to describe his charm. It lay not only in his voice, soft and modulated, not only in his conversation which was often witty, for those who had never heard him speak but had only looked upon him from a distance were aware of a kind of magnetism about the man.

He was handsome, though in a dark, sardonic way, and perhaps it was only the general impression which could be considered handsome. When one examined the features in detail, faults were very visible. The mouth was too large and too loose, the nose too prominent; the cheeks were sunken and the complexion too dark. But in general he gave the impression of good looks. His eyes were dark and luminous, and afterwards Tom came to believe that it was in the eyes that the man's charm lay, for in them was usually a warm, welcoming expression which caused those about him to believe that they and they alone were interesting his Majesty at that moment.

As Tom, Dr. Chubb and Samuel Pepys entered the private gallery, the king was sitting at his ease on a window-seat, a spaniel in his arms, another frisking on the floor at his feet. Charles was fondling the dog on his lap, smoothing the silky ears and murmuring endearments. As the visitors entered, however, he looked up, smiled and rose to his feet courteously, putting down the animal.

"So, it is Mr. Pepys," he said smoothly. "We welcome you, sir, warmly." As the three men bowed, he turned to Chubb. "You are Dr. Chubb? We have much to thank you for, sir, you and your colleagues who braved the plague last year. You strove mightily. Mr. Pepys already knows that I am grateful to him for his efforts as Clerk of the Acts. A brave fellow, egad, is Mr. Pepys, for he spurned danger and remained in London. He has more courage than I, sir !"

Pepys flushed both with pleasure and embarrassment, and swept another bow.

"I would strive even more mightily for a good word from your Majesty," he said.

A sudden smile crossed the king's lips; whether it was without malice, Tom could not have said with any certainty. Nor had he time to wonder, for Charles turned to him.

"Mr. Raynor, I bid you welcome. Your father fought for mine, and thus are we for ever friends. 'Twas at Naseby that he fell?"

The boy knew that Charles must have acquired this information with the sole purpose of seeming

courteous; that he could not have known—or knowing have remembered—John Raynor. And yet such
a realization did not spoil his pleasure in the king's
words. Charles II had done very little for the faithful squires and small landowners who had fought
for his father. Perchance he could not reward them,
however willing to do so, but the fact remained that
the Raynors had impoverished themselves for the
sake of the martyred Charles I, and had received
no reward. Yet Tom was conscious of no malice but
rather of gratitude as he bowed low. For the time
being he really believed that the king had a personal
interest in him.

"An it were necessary, your Majesty, my family
would fight again, for the same cause," he said.

The king laughed, but this time there was no hint
of malice.

"You have the making of a courtier, Mr.
Raynor," he replied. "I am surrounded by fools who
tell me pretty lies—but you are no fool, nor do
you lie, I think."

He went back to the window-seat and picked
up the spaniel again. The three men stood before
him, Tom's eyes glancing round the panelled walls
and carved ceiling. The gallery was one of the private apartments of the palace at Whitehall, and was
frequently used by the king for interviews of a
nature which did not necessitate the extreme privacy
of other chambers at his disposal. It was a gracious
room, the tall windows opening on to lawns and
flower-beds. Through the half-open lattices the boy
could see splashes of colour against green grass; he
could see a girl and a man walking slowly across the

turf, the girl tall and slender, the man exquisitely
dressed in the extravagant fashion of the court.
They were holding hands, and as he watched, Tom
Raynor compressed his lips. Jennifer, Jennifer
Tybald . . . the girl on the lawn reminded him of
her. Jennifer . . . changed so utterly in a few hours.

Two days had elapsed since the incident in the
alley in Pudding Lane, and during that time he had
not set eyes on the girl, though twice he had walked
past her house. The interval had not served to
decrease either his bewilderment or his hurt. Why
had she treated him so? What had happened in the
few hours between walking with her to Mark Lane
and meeting her in Pudding Lane to change her so
utterly? Or had she but toyed with him during the
afternoon, amused herself with him, as maids sometimes did? Tom's eyes grew hard at the thought . . .
and yet he could have sworn, could still swear, that
she had been sincere on the first occasion. And on
the second? Her attitude baffled him, but he could
not bring himself to believe that he had imagined
the change in her, or that she had been but jesting.
Her voice had carried conviction. She had wanted
nothing less in the world than to speak with him or
have him near to her.

The king was speaking again, to Pepys.

"You must be feeling happy, Mr. Pepys, at the
news brought out of Holland. Report has it that over
a hundred Dutch merchantmen have been burned
by Mr. Holmes. That is true, I trust? You have
further news?"

Pepys glowed with pleasure. It was indeed true
that Captain Robin Holmes had audaciously

bearded the enemy in their lair and had burned fat merchantmen lying between Vlieland and the main Dutch coast.

"'Twas a hundred and fifty, your Majesty, and that upon certain word. You may place the damage inflicted upon the enemy at a million pounds sterling."

Charles nodded. The fortunes of war in this fight with the Dutch swayed hither and thither. First, at the Battle of Lowestoft, in the previous year, the English had defeated the enemy heavily; then had come the reverse in the Four Days' Battle, and the triumph of the Dutch, who had sailed victoriously at the mouth of the Thames itself. Now the enemy had suffered great loss at Vlieland.

"'Tis a matter for rejoicing," murmured Charles. "But we must be on our guard, Mr. Pepys. The Dutch are not easily beaten. Look to the navy, sir, and England will always be safe."

He paused, staring out of the window, and then turning, spoke abruptly.

"Well, Mr. Raynor, and you, doctor, what is this tale of treasure that I hear from Mr. Pepys? He has come to me with a rigmarole not dissimilar to that which he brought to me three years ago. What say you, is it another mare's nest?"

Pepys, attacked at his most vulnerable point— his self-conceit—spoke quickly.

"Your Majesty, I but attempted to bring you wealth," he protested. "'Twas a matter attempted in all good faith."

Charles smiled good-humouredly.

"I did not think any other," he said. "Wealth . . .

by my faith, that is urgently needed by the poorest man in the three kingdoms, sirs! That man is I, King of England, yet commanded by my most faithful Commons! They would have me on leading-strings, and like a father disciplining an unruly son, keep me short of money, for thus they think I can come to little harm." He laughed sardonically. "Nor, by my troth, do they make an error in that judgment! Bring me money, Mr. Raynor, and you shall have my lasting gratitude. Yea, and that shall not be your only reward."

Tom's reply was quick. He desired no reward, and as for the possibility that this whole business was a mare's nest, he had no proof one way or the other.

"We but know what Mr. Pepys has already told you, your Majesty. My father certainly had the keeping of some wealth before Naseby field. Whether he indeed left instructions for its discovery, whether the treasure has since been found, whether the rascal Hewitt succeeded in laying hands on the papers, we know not. We may only guess. My father's papers, which Mr. Pepys had in his possession, were stolen, but we cannot say whether they contained those in which we are interested."

There was silence after this forthright statement. The king continued to stroke the spaniel. At last he spoke.

"So . . so. And what of our firebrands? I speak of Kenton and Cocker. You verily believe that they have a hand in the affair?"

Tom did not reply, for he had little inclination to accuse those who were regarded as the king's friends. Pepys, however, took up the tale.

"'Tis likely, your Majesty," he said. "The man Hewitt, as I told your Majesty, was followed to their house and is now their servant."

"Is this true, Mr. Raynor?"

The boy bowed.

"It is true, your Majesty."

Charles pursed his lips, and leaning down, spoke to the spaniel, apparently oblivious of all else but the dog. Then he ceased his endearments.

"And you would have me recover these papers?" he enquired. "'Tis impossible. This matter must not be made public, nor must any know that I am implicated. My faithful Commons, should they hear of this, will do all in their power to rob me of my own."

He laughed bitterly, and he had some reason for bitterness. He had returned to England at the urgent request of those same Commons, who saw in him their only salvation. Once he had assumed the throne, however, they showed their gratitude by attempting to thwart and curb him in every direction.

"So, an I would lay hands on a penny of this wealth, if indeed it exists," continued Charles, "none must know of the affair, nor must any know that I have an interest in it. Kenton and Cocker will remain silent so long as they believe that they themselves can discover this hoard. A word from me, and they will spread the tale abroad."

He gazed at the three men, and his lips were smiling, though little humour showed in his eyes.

"I have very few friends," he said, "and those that I have men try to take from me."

Tom glanced at Dr. Chubb, hitherto silent. The latter's belief that Kenton and Cocker had his Majesty's confidence was evidently wrong. Charles had clearly indicated that he did not regard them as friends, but was aware that like the vast majority of those about him they played their own hands. But if the king could not or would not make a move to regain the papers, it would not be possible to discover the whereabouts of the treasure at Naseby.

"'Tis certain that they have made no move as yet," murmured Chubb slowly, "for both are still in London."

The king put the spaniel back on to the floor and rose to his feet.

"Is it, then, beyond your ingenuity to recover the papers?" he enquired. "Tomorrow our firebrands will be at Whitehall . . . that I can promise you, for I shall bid them come. From seven o'clock in the evening until midnight they will . . . they will not be at Mark Lane, that I can assure you, Mr. Raynor."

Tom was startled, for though Charles had not said as much, the implication contained in his words was very clear. It was a clear incitement to enter the Mark Lane house.

"So, gentlemen, the audience is at an end," said Charles, the dismissal clear. "You have my permission to seek the treasure, but I can give you no warrant. You must trust me . . . even as I trust you. I do not think you will seek to divert it to your own ends."

They bowed and retreated, leaving the king to stare out of the window. At last he turned away and spoke to his dog.

"So, Carlos, we will see," he murmured. "What think you, my friend? Is there indeed treasure, or is it but a mare's nest?"

The spaniel wagged its tale, and Charles laughed.

"You think it true? Perchance it is . . . perchance it is not. But we kings must be wary, Carlos. But you know that, don't you? Very wary. I will have no open hand in this affair."

.   .   .   .   .

"So, Mr. Raynor, you have heard of Kircher? 'Tis possible . . . nay, more than possible. I believe it to be true. If it is. . . ."

Dr. Michael Creid stopped in his pacing and stared at Tom with bright eyes. His usually pallid face was slightly flushed, and his hands were trembling as they clasped and unclasped. The boy had the impression that the young man, though addressing him, was unaware of his existence, that he was talking at him rather than to him.

"Yes, if it is, then what honour to the man who first proves it! Worms . . . so small that the human eye cannot see them. But we now have the new eye, the microscope they call it. I can procure one to use . . . I must procure one. Honour . . . not worldly honour, but——"

Tom broke in, staring at Creid, realizing with even greater force that he was not normal. It was nearly seven o'clock on the evening which was to see Kenton and Cocker dine in private with his Majesty . . . which was to see other events, too, though the admirals did not as yet know that. The hours of this important day had passed slowly for Tom Raynor. His plans were laid as far as they could be, and when darkness fell he was to make his way to the house in Mark Lane and there attempt to secure possession of the property filched by Ezekiel Hewitt.

Thus the hours had passed slowly, and Tom had almost welcomed the present conversation with Dr. Creid on the Italian doctor's theories about the manner in which the plague was carried. The discussion had already served to pass some considerable time, and to take the boy's thoughts away from the task he was about to attempt.

"You really think, then, that the plague does not come from the earth?" he asked.

As though suddenly aware that he had a companion, Michael's eyes focused upon Tom.

"Dr. Hodges is a fool," he said, "and worse than a fool. But I will prove him wrong, prove it for all men to see. Then, perchance, this city will turn from its evil ways and praise the Lord. Yea, praise Him in the heights."

Again Tom felt uncomfortable, as will most Englishmen in such circumstances. He disregarded the outburst.

"How will you prove it?" he enquired. "Can anything draw the worms to the surface, think you? Leeches, perchance?"

He was genuinely interested in the subject, and often thought that he would like to be a doctor—though he doubted whether he had the necessary courage. At Stanton he had spent much time in

poring over the medical treatises which had been
sent to him from London.

"How will I prove it? I will . . ."

Creid broke off abruptly. His face had become
pallid once more; in his eyes, which burned
strangely, suspicion clearly showed.

"I am going," he said, "I am already late. I give
you good-evening, sir."

Swiftly he turned on his heel and left the chamber, meeting his senior partner on the threshold. He
gave him no greeting but passed on. Chubb stared
after him, and then glanced at Tom.

"Has there been trouble between you?" he
murmured. "I warned you, lad, that he might not
take your acquaintance with Mistress Jennifer
kindly."

"We did not speak of her. We talked but of the
plague."

Tom's voice was curt, and Chubb wisely did not
pursue the subject. Instead he spoke of the evening's
expedition.

"Is your mind indeed set on it?" he asked. "Do
you fully understand the risk you run, Tom?"

"Aye . . . and I go alone, Sam. 'Tis better so,
and 'tis my responsibility. As for the risk, they
cannot deny me entrance, I think. After that,
'tis a question of fortune. Do not worry, Sam,
but those papers I will have if it is humanly
possible."

The doctor shrugged his shoulders, but made
no further attempt to dissuade him. Youth, as he
knew, was not easily turned from its chosen path. He
had some hope, however, that Tom would not gain

entrance to the house in Mark Lane, for it was likely that since the incident when Tom had accused Ezekiel of theft, the servants would have been given orders not to admit him.

As it happened, however, this hope was in vain. Whether it was that Kenton and Cocker had not anticipated such audacity and had thus given no orders to the servants, or whether Tom's commanding manner was sufficient to overawe the servant who opened the door to him, the fact remained that at ten o'clock, by which time it was dark, he was admitted to the admirals' house in Mark Lane. The servant assured him that neither Kenton nor Cocker was expected from Whitehall until late, but Tom waved the objection aside.

"My business with your masters is urgent," he said briefly. "They will not be pleased if I do not await them."

"I will bring you wine, sir," said the servant, and Tom, though he might well need every moment he could secure, did not make the mistake of refusing the refreshment. The man came with the wine in a few minutes, and Tom waited for some little time before he made his first move. Ezekiel Hewitt, now in the admiral's employ, might at any moment discover who had thus entered the house; and there were also Rumbold and Clewitt, both of whom were aware that their masters had no liking for Thomas Raynor. As he gently opened the door of the room, therefore, Tom was fully aware that any one of these three might make a sudden appearance and ruin his plans. It was a risk, however, which had to be taken.

Fortune was with him. The passage outside was empty. Twenty yards away was the room in which he had interviewed Kenton and Cocker, a room obviously used as a private closet. To the door of his chamber Tom glided silently. It was unlocked. Cautiously he opened it and slipped inside the room. Scarcely was he across the threshold when he heard footsteps approaching along the passage outside; and before he had time to hide, the door of the chamber opened for the second time within the space of moments. Holding a candlestick, Ezekiel Hewitt stood staring at him.

The emergency was upon Tom before he had time to plan how to meet it. But if he was surprised, the intruder was more so. Thus Tom had a few seconds' grace, and he used them to good effect. Before Ezekiel had well taken in the significance of his sudden appearance, the boy had leaped. The candlestick was swept to the floor, and two strong hands grasped the fellow round the throat. He fell, Tom on top of him. Ezekiel was no match for his assailant, and his weak efforts to dislodge him were unavailing.

Tom's grip tightened on his throat, and the rogue's senses reeled. And as he knelt on him Tom was wondering how long it would be before somebody came, drawn thither by the noise. Strangely, however, none came, and with a thrill Tom realized that this part of the house must be deserted, and that he had Ezekiel Hewitt at his mercy.

He released his grip slightly, though pinning Ezekiel firmly still. His voice rasped in his erstwhile servant's ear.

"You know what I seek, fellow. The papers you stole from Seething Lane. Where are they?"

It was but a slender chance that the rogue knew where his new masters had secreted the documents, but scarce were the words spoken than Tom knew that the millionth chance had eventuated. He could but dimly discern Ezekiel, for in the fracas the door had closed, and the candle had fallen, so that the room was in darkness. But there was that slight stiffening of Ezekiel's limbs, that sudden tenseness which proved that he did indeed know something of the papers.

"I—I know nothing," he quavered, his voice hardly audible. "I—I swear. . . ."

Tom said nothing for a moment. Holding him with one hand easily enough, he fumbled for his dagger and drew it. The point was sharp and cold against his victim's throat.

"Speak," said the boy, "or by the saints you die."

His voice carried conviction, and Ezekiel, not the bravest of men, capitulated without further argument.

"I will show you," he muttered.

Tom released him, and allowed him to rise. He realized that he was taking a great risk, but there was no other practicable course. Ezekiel might well stake all in raising his voice for assistance, but . . . the risk must be accepted. The dagger held firmly against the fellow's back, Tom forced him to strike flame from tinder-box and light the candle. Ezekiel made no attempt to escape or to call for help; evidently he implicitly believed that to do so would be to court instant death, though Tom himself knew that he could not kill in cold blood. He was thankful, however, that the threat had sounded so convincing.

"Now, the papers," he said grimly.

Ezekiel turned and shuffled across the room, Tom close behind him, the dagger touching the rascal. In his other hand the boy held the candlestick.

Thus they came to a door set in the wall of the chamber, and Ezekiel drew out a key. Whether he had it unlawfully or with the knowledge of his masters, Tom neither knew nor cared. The door swung open, revealing a second room, smaller than the first. It was empty, though for a moment Tom had wondered whether he was being led into a trap.

"In there," muttered Ezekiel, pointing to a small iron chest which stood by the farther wall.

"Open it," was the curt instruction. If Ezekiel had hoped that his captor, eager to obtain the papers, would fling caution to the winds, he was mistaken. Reluctantly he knelt, inserted another key and opened the lid of the chest. Then he hesitated, but Tom, pressing forward, touched the bare skin of his throat with the sharp point of the dagger. The man cowered away. He fumbled in the chest—and in another moment Tom had a small packet of papers in his hands. One glance was sufficient to identify his father's hand. On the top of the packet was a paper at which he stared greedily, for his eyes had caught a few words—a few vital words.

Twenty paces north of the north-east buttress. . .

He had found what he had come to seek. Even as he stared, a voice sounded from the passage.

"Halloa, there, who. . . ."

E

The rest was lost, for Tom acted urgently. Whoever had called was even now entering the other room. Tom pushed Ezekiel away, against the wall, dashed the candlestick to the ground and ran for the door which led into the other chamber —the only door in the inner closet. On the threshold he collided with a large, heavy man. His fist came out and struck. The man reeled away. Swiftly Tom ran across the room, found the window, unlatched it and without hesitation swung through. He dropped some eight feet, landed on his toes and was away, up the alley into which the side-door opened, and which previously he had seen Ezekiel use. From behind him he heard shouts, but in another few moments he was into Mark Lane and was lost in the darkness. He clutched the packet of papers fiercely.

CHAPTER VIII

In Which the Admirals first Bicker and then Agree

IT was dark, but a small moon rode the sky, and its dim light touched the muddle of broken masonry and blackened timbers which marked where Bury Manor had once stood in all its graciousness. Twenty years had elapsed since the Parliamentary forces, after the victory at Naseby, had burned the house and left their work to be completed by nature's ruthless hand.

The owners of Bury Manor had fled to France soon after the Battle of Naseby and had never returned to reclaim their heritage and rebuild their home. Now, after twenty desolate years, giant creepers had grown over some of the scattered stone blocks which littered the site, bushes showed within the walls, the grass of the park had grown coarse and rank and had encroached with every passing year upon the ruined manor. None came near Bury Manor nowadays, unless occasionally the villagers of the neighbouring hamlet of Naseby used the park as a short-cut—and they never approached it after dark. It was said, as is so often of ruins, that it was haunted.

Thus in silent decay stood the ruins of Bury Manor, stone huddled upon broken stone, timbers lying athwart them, still black from the fire which the vandals had lit; and over all hung the desolation which decay must always bring. The trees whispered mournfully together as the night breeze touched their leaves; an owl hooted from its lair amongst the broken stones; and within the walls a dim light flickered as men moved stealthily to and fro with lanthorns. On this late August night Bury was not so deserted as it usually was, and had any villager braved its desolation he could have told a tale of undeniable haunting.

Five men were within the precincts of Bury Manor, three busy with picks and ropes, the other two looking on. These latter, stout gentlemen, well cloaked, were arguing vehemently, and though they attempted to subdue their voices, from time to time nature won, and they fell to shouting.

"Twenty paces," snorted Admiral Kenton, "twenty paces, fool! Does it not say so plainly enough?"

Admiral Cocker controlled his temper—slightly.

"Twenty paces it says," he rasped, "but from the north-east buttress, sir. I am not assured that——"

"Ha, landlubberly dog!" exploded his companion. "Do you not know north from south? I can well believe it, by the saints!"

Cocker's hand flew to his sword hilt, while Kenton, stepping back to give himself more room, brought his own sword half out of its sheath. For the moment neither gentleman had any interest in this search for a king's treasure, or even in the fact that others also seeking it might well be on their heels and might arrive at almost any moment. Kenton and Cocker had squabbled and bickered for too many years to be able to deny the course of what had become nature, though their very lives had depended upon it. A matter for much wonder was it that they were able to live together, under the same roof; but it was likely that had they been separated, both would have died of sheer boredom!

Kenton's blade was half out of its sheath, but it was never fully drawn, for at that moment a dark shape flitted to his side, and the rascal Ezekiel spoke low.

"Your honour, someone comes!"

Back went the blade into the sheath, and Cocker, too, consented to forget that he had been insulted. Complete silence fell on Bury Manor, as those who had been working with picks ceased their efforts, and the two admirals and Ezekiel strained their eyes across the dark park.

None knew better than they that there was every chance that they would be disturbed at their work. They did not fear interruption from the villagers, who gave the manor a wide berth after dark; but interference from others was a very real peril. Upon learning from Ezekiel that Tom Raynor had visited the house in Mark Lane, and had secured his father's papers, Kenton and Cocker had wasted no further time, but had taken coach for Naseby early the next morning. They had reached Bury Manor first, but it might well be only a matter of an hour or so before those who might well consider that they had a better claim than the admirals to the papers—and thus to the treasure —arrived on the scene.

It was difficult to decide whether Kenton or Cocker had been the more angry when the discovery was made that the papers had gone. Ezekiel, whose glib tongue and crafty brain had stood him in good stead in that he had found no difficulty in presenting a plausible tale which made no mention that he himself had succumbed to the threat of force and had revealed the hiding-place of the papers, was thankful that his new masters did not know the full story. They were angry enough already, cursing Ezekiel and the other two servants who were more or less in their confidence—though Rumbold and Clewitt did not then know all the facts—for permitting the rogue Raynor to enter the house and break open the chest. Had they known the facts, it was likely that in the heat of the moment they would have assaulted Ezekiel.

"But your honours," whined the rascal, "little harm has been done. We have a copy of the paper, and now we may have Mr. Raynor taken on a charge of theft."

"Little harm done, egad! By all the saints, is the fellow out of Bedlam? Have Raynor taken! And thus have this affair made public? Pah, you're a fool! Little harm! Will not this accursed Raynor ride straight for Naseby? Or think you he will lie abed dreaming? Pah!"

The tedious journey into Northamptonshire had been enlivened by incessant bickering, the argument to which they returned ever and anon concerning whether the blame for not commencing the journey some days earlier, when the papers had first come into their possession, should rest on Kenton's shoulders or on Cocker's.

Cocker swore—most vehemently and pictur-

esquely—that it had been Kenton who had insisted
on remaining until after they had dined with his
Majesty, an honour which they had known to be
imminent; Kenton maintained quite as picturesquely
that it had been Cocker who had wanted to talk
privately with the king. The argument was never
settled. Both gentlemen desired all that they could
squeeze out of his Majesty, and neither had wanted
to be away from London when the expected sum-
mons arrived, though neither would admit as much.
It was a fact, too, that for all their professed loyalty,
neither Kenton nor Cocker had the least intention
of informing Charles of the discovery of the treasure
—if indeed they discovered it—and had no suspicion
that their opponents had already explained the affair
to his Majesty.

"'Tis nothing. Back to your task, man,"
snorted Kenton at last, after they had remained still
and silent for nearly ten minutes, and had been
rewarded only by the sound of rustling trees and
hooting owls. "None comes," he added.

Ezekiel glided away, and the two admirals followed him, their argument regarding the points of
the compass temporarily abandoned.

The three servants were working at a point some
fifty yards away, and had already lifted two of the
great flags which paved the weed-ridden courtyard.
Twenty paces away the buttress which Kenton
maintained was that mentioned in John Raynor's
instructions, still reared its bulk, though the flank-
ing walls were crumbling into ruin. The two
gentlemen halted and watched in silence, while
Rumbold, in charge of the operations, gave instruc-

tions for Clewitt to take pick and spade and break
the earth under the flag. The man obeyed, and
worked steadily for fifteen minutes, at the end of
which time no reward for hard work had been
achieved. Then Ezekiel took the spade, and worked
for another five minutes, while the pile of earth
above him gradually increased.

"'Tis certain that you have the wrong buttress,"
said Cocker at last. "I told you, sir, that . . ."

He was interrupted by an exclamation from
Ezekiel, whose spade had chinked on something
hard and metallic. In another moment the earth had
been scraped away from the lid of a small chest,
measuring two feet long by eighteen inches wide.

"By the saints, we have struck!" exclaimed
Kenton, and the two admirals most unaccountably
found themselves shaking hands.

"Quick man, to work!" exclaimed Cocker,
exhorting the perspiring Ezekiel, "to work!"

It was not easy to unearth the rest of the chest,
which was of iron and some twelve inches deep, but
at last ropes were placed round it and it was hauled
to the surface. The lock had rusted through, for the
earth here was very damp, even in the summer; and
a single blow from an iron bar broke the now flimsy
catch. Kenton reached down and flung open the lid
—and there, before their eyes was very proof that
neither Old Ben nor John Raynor had lied. Carefully wrapped in cloth already beginning to fall
apart, was wealth of which it was difficult to assess
the value at this first hurried inspection; but there
were silver cups and plates, and there was gold
glinting yellow in the light of the lanthorns, the gold

not only of plate and goblets, but of coins breaking through the cloth bags which held them now so precariously.

There was silence while the five men peered and handled; the silence of astonishment that they should have succeeded in the search, and of greed. The two admirals gazed covetously at the treasure, while Ezekiel's eyes glistened at the sight.

"We must be gone," said Kenton at last. "Every moment spent here spells danger. Get the chest to the coach."

Using the ropes the chest was dragged to the coach which had been brought after dark to within a few yards of the ruins, and after some difficulty was hoisted inside. It was fortunately not large, and though heavy it was possible to lift it by the aid of the ropes. The chest deposited, the two admirals climbed into the vehicle, and thus they lumbered away from Bury Manor.

They passed through Naseby village without halting, and did not pause until they reached Farthingale, some ten miles beyond Naseby in the direction of London. Rumbold drove, with Ezekiel next to him, and Clewitt escorted the coach, riding his horse with pistol ready drawn. No road in England was safe after dark, and it would indeed have been a calamity had any gentleman of the road decided to hold up this particular coach! Clewitt, who like Rumbold, had served under Kenton at sea, was likely to give better than he received, however, in the event of an attack, and Rumbold himself was a man of great strength and experience in warfare.

The admirals felt safe enough as the heavy vehicle lumbered over the uneven roads.

Arrived at Farthingale the coach stopped at an inn, and Ezekiel hurried to bid mine host prepare a meal for the exalted passengers. The sight of the livery, evidence that gentlemen of quality had condescended to make use of The Red Lion, was sufficient to set the landlord hurrying and scurrying; if he thought it strange that the passengers remained in the coach until the meal was ready, and that then only one at a time ate, leaving the other still in the coach, he made no comment. Gentlemen of quality were frequently eccentric. It was none of his business.

While the food was preparing, Kenton and Cocker occupied themselves in transferring the contents of the chest to a leather trunk, far lighter than the iron chest. The result was that the treasure could now easily be handled by two men without undue fatigue. The iron chest could be disposed of along the road to London. Their task completed, first Kenton and then Cocker descended for refreshment, the coach thus never being left unattended, the servants, too, taking it in turns to eat. Within an hour all was done, and the coach was ready to resume its journey, the horses having been changed, and Clewitt also being remounted.

Ezekiel Hewitt, who had been bidden to eat last, quaffed his ale, rose to his feet and walked out of the inn. His little eyes were cunning. The treasure had been found; now all that remained was to ensure that . . . He stopped suddenly on the threshold of the main doorway. The coach, drawn up outside, was beginning to move. Rumbold, on the box, was shaking the reins . . . the horses were straining in the shafts. Ezekiel, not yet realizing the intention, ran forward, shouting. No notice was taken, except that Clewitt, turning in the saddle, waved his gloved hand in mocking farewell. Then a head was thrust out of the coach window, and Admiral Kenton's voice could be heard urging Rumbold to greater efforts.

Ezekiel came to a halt as the coach drew out of the courtyard. Fool that he had been not to realize that this simple expedient might be used to jettison him! Cursed fool to have been so easily hood-winked! So occupied had he been in laying his own plans to secure the treasure after Kenton and Cocker had converted it into coin, that he had not realized that the two admirals might also be laying their plans to avoid sharing the wealth with him. Ezekiel Hewitt swore fluently as he stood and helplessly watched coach and horseman turn out of the yard and clatter out of view. The last sight Clewitt had of him was his white face, distorted with rage, illuminated by the light which streamed from the open doorway.

As for Kenton and Cocker, they knew an unwonted peace during the tedious journey to Lon-don. It was a long time since they had not argued for such a lengthy space, and though no doubt by the next day they would be bickering again, for the time being their satisfaction at discovering the treasure and jettisoning Ezekiel Hewitt sufficed to keep them both in good temper.

"Scuppered, by gad," murmured Kenton,

leaning back in the coach and gazing at the trunk containing the plate and gold. "Scuppered, by the Lord!"

Cocker nodded, chuckling. Rumbold and Clewitt had often enough proved their loyalty in the past, and neither admiral feared that they would lay information with the authorities or attempt to seize any part of the hoard to convert it to their own use. They would be suitably rewarded for their assistance, and would undoubtedly be satisfied. As for gossiping, the two ex-sailors were noted for their taciturnity.

There was only one fly in the ointment—Tom Raynor, and his friend Dr. Samuel Chubb, knew more than it was expedient for them to know. They would reach Bury Manor to find the hoard gone, and evidence that it had been unearthed. They would return to London convinced that Kenton and Cocker had seized it. Proof would be lacking, but it would perhaps be wise not to take the treasure to Mark Lane. Once already a successful entry had been effected by Tom Raynor; a second would be disastrous, and though in theory it should be simple enough to prevent it, in practice it would not be so simple. The admirals did not wish to live for ever on tenterhooks, always on guard.

It was Cocker who provided an alternative. In Pudding Lane lived Faryner, the baker, a man under obligation to them. Why not use his services?

"The fellow will ask no questions," said Cocker, "and for a consideration will be glad to oblige us. The trunk will be safe enough with him. And remember, there was the incident of the robbery. We have a hold over him and he will not dare to break trust."

Kenton considered. It was true that Faryner was under obligation to them, especially as he would yet go to the gallows at a word from Cocker, who by chance had stumbled upon proof that the rogue had been implicated in a street robbery a year before.

Kenton felt that it was against his principles to agree with Cocker, but on this occasion . . .

"You have the truth of it," he growled at last. "We will take the trunk to Faryner's, and leave it there until such time as the puppy Raynor grows tired of searching for it. The hoard has lain hid twenty years—another few weeks will not hurt it."

And so, during the next night, when Pudding Lane was in darkness, Faryner took into his custody a certain trunk, swore by all the saints to keep it safe . . . and fully intended to keep his word. He had no desire to adorn the gallows.

CHAPTER IX

In Which a Conspiracy is Revealed

EVERYTHING had failed. As Tom rode with Chubb through the streets of London on this afternoon of August 31st, his thoughts were bitter. The expedition to Naseby had failed, only by a matter of hours, perchance, but this was sufficient and more than sufficient. And Jennifer Tybald was beyond his reach, not only because it was her father's will that she should marry Michael Creid, but evidently by her own wish. That was the bitterest pill to swallow. Time counted for nothing; had he known her for twenty years he could not love her more than he did now. And he had thought . . . fool that he had been to think at all ! She had but played with him, amused herself in his company for an hour, and he, like any country yokel, had imagined that she cared for him. In grim silence he rode through the capital, for the second time within the space of a fortnight riding into London from the country. But on this occasion he felt no interest in the sights of the city, for he was immersed in his own unhappy thoughts.

The packet of papers so miraculously retrieved from Mark Lane, Tom and Sam had wasted no time in leaving London, and though they had not known it at the time, they had left the capital within a few hours of Kenton and Cocker taking coach to Naseby. Well mounted, and travelling far more lightly, they had outstripped the cumbersome coach, and would have reached Naseby well in advance of their opponents had not bad fortune dogged their steps.

Riding across an open moor, they came suddenly upon a sheltered dell where a small fire burned wanly, over which crouched a man and a woman, the latter holding in her arms a child. Tom and Sam would have passed by the vagrants, had it not been that Sam was a doctor, and his keen eye saw that the child was ill. Reining in, he had swung from the saddle, and with reassuring words, for the man had cowered away and the woman had clutched the child closely to her, had made an examination.

When at last he stood back, Tom had spoken.

"Not the plague, Sam?"

"No, but the child will die an it does not have care."

Then once again Tom had been given cause to marvel at Dr. Samuel Chubb. Wealthy though he was, and a gentleman, it apparently did not occur to him to leave the child to its fate. He elicited from the man that he was an ex-sailor, turned away from the fleet some three years before without any pay— as was common enough—and since living upon scraps and pieces, hunted from one parish to another, the authorities being eager to avoid any responsibility, and thus hounding all vagrants on . . . ever on. Through the fellow's ragged shirt could be seen old weals, where the authorities had whipped him for no other crime than his inability to support himself except by begging. It was pitiful enough, but also common enough. Chubb, however, was interested only in saving life. His money commanded obedience, and within two hours the vagrants had been lodged at an inn a mile or so away, at Farthingale, and the child had been cared for.

It was not until the next day that the doctor would agree to continue the journey to Naseby. Before he left the inn he handed mine host gold, and gave instructions that the vagrants were to be housed and fed for two weeks, at the end of which time the child should be well again. He also intimated that he himself would return to see that his instructions were being carried out.

Thus eight hours had been lost; and those hours were of vital importance. Arrived at Bury Manor they had found a multitude of evidence that John Raynor had laid no false trail; there, gaping wide, was the pit from which the treasure chest had been taken, and in the soft earth of the overgrown drive were the marks of a coach's wheels. It required no effort to deduce that Kenton and Cocker had stolen a march on them, and evidence was quickly obtained, for the admirals had been seen in Naseby itself, and it was easy enough to identify them from the descriptions provided by residents.

For a little Tom had been bitter that the beggar's child should have thus delayed them and made it possible for Kenton and Cocker to secure the treasure. But then, gradually, the boy had realized that he was behaving badly. The child was a vagrant's child, but that did not alter the fact that a life had been at stake. Tom had reviled the ill-fortune which had caused the delay; he soon realized, however, that it was not ill but good fortune which had led them across the moor that afternoon. He remembered the dumb gratitude in the vagrant's lean face, and the incredulous joy in the woman's eyes.

It was as they neared London on their return that Tom stammered his apologies to Chubb. He had not actually stated that the doctor should not have wasted time over the child, but he was fully aware that he had implied as much. Sam smiled tolerantly.

"Let us not talk of it," he said. "I am sorry that we were too late, but . . . I am a doctor, lad." And then, slowly, "Life makes its demands, and it brings its rewards. That you will discover for yourself as you grow older."

Later the boy was to remember these words, and wonder that they should have been spoken so appositely. Revisiting the inn where the vagrants had been housed, they had learned that the woman and child still remained there, but that the man had gone, none knew whither or for what purpose. The woman herself professed ignorance, and the landlord had been fervid in his plea that the fellow had insisted on going and could not be dissuaded. Sam had paid him more gold and had gone his way, neither he nor Tom realizing—as how should they? —that the lank-haired sailor, who called himself William Glover, was to cross their path again, in dramatic fashion.

As he rode by Sam's side through the city, Tom no longer reviled the ill-fortune which had decreed the delay, but his thoughts were still bitter. The treasure had been filched almost from under their very noses, and thus had disappeared all hopes of arousing his Majesty's gratitude. Tom was but human, and he had hoped that if he were successful at Bury Manor, Charles might have assisted him in his difficult task of administering the Market Stanton estate. Money was woefully lacking. Even a little assistance would have been welcome. And there was Jennifer. . . .

At the top of Seething Lane he parted from Chubb, having no desire to accompany his friend in search of Mr. Pepys.

He then made his solitary way to Lombard Street, leaving Sam to go to the Navy Office. As he rode the short distance between the two streets, his thoughts alternated between the lost treasure and Jennifer Tybald. Why had she taken the trouble to amuse herself with him? Why had she gone out of her way to pretend that she was attracted when all the time she had no interest in him? And why had she been so bitter when he had seen her that night in Pudding Lane? The fact that she had but passed an idle hour in his company, had amused herself with him, was surely no reason why she should be so hard, so bitter when next she saw him. He remembered the furtive figures which had entered William Tybald's house on that same night. Had they anything to do with the girl's attitude? It was surely impossible, and yet. . . .

His thoughts still concerned with the girl, it was with something of a shock that upon entering the doctor's house in Lombard Street he should come immediately face to face with Michael Creid.

"Dr. Chubb will not be long," he began. "I left

him but a few minutes since. We have but now returned from the country."

Creid knew nothing of their real object in journeying into Northamptonshire, but had merely been informed that they had to travel thither on private business. Tom had been but making conversation, but when Creid did not reply, and seemed hardly to have heard him, he looked at him more closely. It was surely strange that he should take so little interest in Chubb's affairs.

"You have been in good health, I trust?" murmured Tom, noting that Michael's face, as pallid as ever, now showed two vivid spots of colour on the cheeks, and that his hair lay lank and uncared for on his shoulders. His garments, too, seemed dirtier than usual, more slipshod, and there was an air of unkemptness about him. He looked ill, and Tom saw that his lips were never still, but were moving as though he whispered to himself.

"Yea, I am well," muttered the young doctor.

"And what of the plague? You have a case in Pudding Lane, have you not?"

At that Creid looked at him wildly, mouthed words which were unintelligible, and without warning sank down on a settle and began to weep. Tom stared down at him in amazement, and despite his loathing, despite the fact that he had no knowledge why Creid should behave thus, felt an instinctive pity welling up in him. The young man was leaning forward, head on his hands, and his body shook convulsively.

Tom touched him on the shoulder.

"Is there anything I can do?" he asked gently.

Creid pushed him away and staggered to his feet. His face was haggard, his eyes wild as he peered at the boy. And in those eyes, Tom was confident, madness stared out nakedly.

"Get ye behind me, Satan," mouthed Creid. "O, God, how long will ye delay? Is not Babylon's time yet come? Have we not sinned enough?"

A quivering finger pointed at Tom; on Creid's lips flecks of foam had appeared.

"Ye spawn of the devil," he cried, "have ye not tempted me enough? In agony she died, yea, in agony, but will yet come to paradise. Get ye gone, Beelzebub, to your father the Devil!"

With that he flung himself from the room, leaving Tom to stare after him, unable to credit the evidence of his own senses. Dr. Michael Creid was mad, of that there could be no doubt. His incoherences could not longer be believed to be merely religious fervour.

Shaken by the experience, Tom went to his own chamber. This madman was to wed Jennifer Tybald! Horrified at the thought, the boy stared out of the window into Lombard Street. The girl could not know that her betrothed was insane, and rapidly growing worse. Did she know, then not for a moment, Tom was convinced, would she contemplate marrying him.

Within a few moments he left the house again, not waiting for Sam to return from Seething Lane. Jennifer had made it clear that she wished to have no more to do with him, but willy-nilly she must listen to what he now had to say. He made his way to Pudding Lane, as yet uncertain how to persuade her to see him. No doubt he could gain entrance to the house easily enough, for Tybald himself was under some obligation to him in respect of the money paid for Old Ben's keep. But once, in, how to speak with the girl alone?

The problem, however, did not arise. He was halfway along the narrow, dirty street, when commotion suddenly broke out in a house a few yards from him. A scream rent the air, and even as Tom halted, startled, Jennifer Tybald appeared at the door of a house. Her face was white, her hair was falling about her face, and as she stood in the doorway she swayed and clutched at the door-post.

Tom was across the street in a flash. He saw that the door of the house bore the fatal plague cross, but he paid no attention to it. Not long since he had passed this same door with revulsion and fear; now he was impervious to fear. His arm went round the girl's shoulder.

"Jennifer, what is it? What has happened?"

She did not draw away from him, but allowed him to hold her. Gradually her breathing became more normal, but she clung to him almost frantically.

"'Tis . . . Michael. He . . . I think he is mad."

"Michael!"

Tom made a movement to enter the house, but she drew him back with unexpected strength.

"No—no, Tom. There is plague. He . . . forced me across the threshold. I—take me away, Tom. Take me away, please."

"Where is Creid now?" he asked, pushing angrily through the little knot of people drawn hither by the girl's scream.

"He is upstairs. Tom, do not delay. Take me away."

She was still distraught, and saying no more, Tom walked with her down Pudding Lane, past her house and so to the river bank. Here they halted.

"My sweet, you must tell me what happened. I came to warn you."

"To warn me?"

He nodded, and briefly explained what had happened at Chubb's house. She drew a deep breath.

"I ... I thank you. I knew he was not as other men are, but I did not know ... until this afternoon. Tom, it was horrible."

He soothed her again, and gradually the tale was told. Creid had come to Pudding Lane not ten minutes earlier, and had asked her to go walking with him. She would have refused, but her father had been present and had insisted that she go. Creid's manner had been strained, and she had been even then a little frightened, but had quelled her fears. Drawing level with the plague house, and the watchman being absent, he had suddenly gripped her arm and before she could resist had swung her through the door. Then she had struggled, but it had taken several minutes before she had managed to release herself. She had screamed, scarcely knowing what she was doing, for Creid had been mouthing incoherencies, foaming at the mouth, and the girl had been terrified. At last she had escaped, and Creid had run upstairs.

"He is mad," said Tom gravely, "and must be

restrained. You did not go near the patient, Jennifer?"

"No, but a few feet across the threshold." She drew away from him. "I would not infect you," she added.

For answer he stretched out his arm and drew her close against him. She said nothing, but she came willingly, and Tom knew that this time she was not playing with him. At last she spoke.

"Tom, the woman in that house is dead. Michael said so. And he raved that he had killed her, and that you had brought him to do it. He said I must go up and see her."

The boy frowned. Something of the same sort the madman had babbled in Lombard Street. It was nonsense . . . unless . . . yes, it was possible that Creid had been experimenting, working on Kircher's theories of worms carrying the infection to human beings. He had, perchance, experimented on this case in Pudding Lane, and the result had been that the woman had died. His mad brain might well have told him that Tom Raynor had first persuaded him to experiment, though in fact it was evident that he had done so even before Tom had spoken of Kircher, or at any rate that he had reached a decision to experiment.

"He but raved," he said quietly. "I know nothing of the case."

"No, of course not." She was silent for a moment, and then, turning to him, spoke in a low voice. "Tom, I am . . . I am sorry. It was wrong of me to speak to you so when I found you in the alley. But I was afraid."

"Afraid, sweetheart? Yea, 'twas dark, and perchance you mistook me for a rogue. There are many such in London. But enough of that. I bear no ill-will, for . . . for I love you, Jennifer."

She nodded gravely. There was no foolish pretence, and no embarrassment visible on her face.

"Yes, that I know."

"And you? Will you have me for husband, sweet?"

Swiftly she turned, and her arms were round his neck. For a long moment they kissed. Then she pushed him gently away."

"Yes, I love you," she said, "though I had thought not to love any man. But . . . there is my father. I do not know what he will say. He is stubborn, Tom, and . . . and foolish."

Her eyes clouded, and a shadow came over her face. Before Tom could speak again she had turned back to him.

"I told you that I was afraid," she said, "but it was not of rogues who rob in the dark and run. I am afraid for my father. On that night . . ."

"Yes, on that night men came to your house," he said quietly, "and they came after dark, furtively. What means it, Jennifer. You may trust me."

"I can trust you," she repeated. "That I know, now. But then I was afraid that you had come to spy, and I spoke harshly and sent you away. Tom, my father . . . conspires against his Majesty."

"Tell me," said Tom quietly.

Jennifer obeyed, and in a quiet voice, which nevertheless did not conceal her anxiety, told him of what she knew, of what she suspected. She was not supposed to know anything, but she was intelligent and had long since guessed that her father was implicated in some unlawful proceeding. Men had come to the house after dark, meetings had been held behind locked doors, conversations had been cut short upon her entering a room. She had watched and listened, and now she knew much, guessed more.

"My father believes that the king is the devil come to earth again," she said. "But Tom, he is not mad, not as Michael is. He was brought up to believe that all kings are evil. He is no murderer, yet he will kill, and killing believe that he is doing the best he can for his country. Can you understand?"

"Yes, I think I can."

This was true, for Tom had imagination, and he knew that twenty years ago Cromwell had commanded men no less fanatical, men who sincerely believed that they were fighting the forces of evil. He knew enough, and had sufficient imagination to realize that a man such as William Tybald, who had served under Cromwell, and had lived for many years under his influence and under that of the Ironsides whose very sincerity had brought them victory, might well believe that the killing of a king was no murder.

"They intend to kill his Majesty?" he asked, and even as he spoke realized how fantastic it was that he should be standing here by the quiet Thames putting such a question to this copper-gold girl.

Her face was deathly white, her voice scarce above a whisper when she answered.

"Yes. They do not suspect that I know. When there are meetings I am sent into Master Faryner's, the baker's, to bear his wife company. But I delay when I can, and I know what they intend. Tom, you must help me, and my father. Your father fought at Naseby against mine, but . . . can you help me and him? He does not realize what he brings upon himself and upon me. And he does not realize that 'tis murder. Faryner persuades him, and there are others."

"Faryner? So he is of the party?"

"Yes. He, too, fought with Cromwell."

Without persuasion she told all that she knew, naming four others who were implicated in the conspiracy. As yet she did not know what date had been fixed for the attempt on the king's life, and it was probable that it had not yet been agreed, for the conspirators intended to seize their opportunity when Charles next went to Windsor.

"Do not worry," he said finally, in gentle tones. "I will not betray them. But you know that. When you learn what date has been agreed, let me know." Then, as he remembered an incident in Tybald's house, on the day after Old Ben had died, he put an abrupt question. "What of Creid? Is he of the company."

"I . . . I am not sure. But it may be so."

He nodded. He was remembering the way in which Tybald had made to interrupt Creid when he had mouthed religious platitudes about evil and sin; and how he had broken in on Faryner's denunciation of the king.

" 'Tis likely that he is," he said. "But do not fret, my sweet. I will do all that can be done. And have a care for yourself."

They parted, and Tom made his slow way back to Lombard Street, deep in thought. It had been easy to reassure Jennifer, to promise that no harm should befall her or her father. But how to implement that promise? The conspiracy could be broken easily enough by laying information, which, in fact, his duty to Charles demanded. But thus William Tybald would come to the gallows . . . and Tom Raynor loved his daughter. Aye, and she loved him. The thought set his heart singing in spite of this new trouble. At all costs he must save her father from himself, and from the gallows or the executioner's block. For treason they disembowelled a man, beheaded him and quartered his body. Tom shuddered from the thought. And there was Jennifer, innocent, but would the authorities believe this? She, too, might . . . Tom's face went white at the thought. Some way must be found. Slowly he walked back up Pudding Lane and so to Lombard Street, where he found Chubb awaiting him.

CHAPTER X

In Which Tom Comes Yet Again to Pudding Lane

"He has not returned?"

Tom put the question anxiously, but knew already that Michael Creid had not yet come back, for Sam's face was grave. It was now more than twenty-four hours since the incident in Pudding Lane, and Chubb's partner was still at large.

"No, not yet. I am worried, Tom, and I blame myself somewhat. As a doctor I should have realized the danger . . . but we rarely see what is under our very noses."

Tom nodded. His attitude to Creid and his absence was frankly selfish. Michael Creid could do what he pleased as far as he cared—except go near Jennifer Tybald again.

Seeing the anxiety on the boy's face, Chubb spoke soothingly.

"I have made it my business to warn Tybald," he said. "The man has a great fondness for his daughter, and will guard her well. You have no cause to fret, Tom."

The boy turned away. No cause to fret! Much cause had he, and his anxiety was not entirely due to Creid's absence and the possibility that he would seek out Jennifer Tybald. That was but one of the dangers that threatened her, and, perchance, the least. Tom would have given much to have been able to confide in Sam, to have been able to tell him of the conspiracy in which William Tybald was so deeply implicated, and which might so easily bring not only himself but his daughter to utter ruin. But it was impossible to confide in anyone, even in Samuel Chubb, a proved friend. It was scarcely possible that Sam would betray Tybald, but to confide in him would be to make him an accessory, and that Tom would not do. He and he alone must find a way to save Jennifer and, if possible, her father from committing suicide—for such it was.

His face was pale with anxiety as desperately he tried to find a way of escape from the maze of circumstance. A sleepless night had done nothing to clear his thoughts, and the morning and afternoon had dragged by without result. A way must be found, but what way was there? To go to Tybald and attempt to dissuade him from the course he had chosen would bring no good result, and might well make matters worse. Tybald and Faryner, and the others implicated, would not abandon their plans, and would therefore be forced to close the mouth of the outsider who had discovered their plot. What could one man do against so many? And there was Jennifer to consider. It would be evident that his information had derived from her; once already Tom had heard Tybald threaten to beat her, and he knew that the Puritan fanatic would not hesitate to sacrifice even his own child to what he considered a just and righteous cause. No, escape did not lie along that path.

Tom's interest in the Bury Manor treasure had

evaporated, and now, when Sam began to speak of his meeting with Mr. Pepys, he found it difficult to pay attention. Sam, however, anxious to dissuade him from brooding over Jennifer's danger, persisted.

Mr. Pepys, immersed though he was in navy business, for the Dutch had put to sea again and Rupert and Monck had hastily put out from Southwold Bay to seek battle, found time to interrupt his labours to listen to the sorry tale. The Clerk of the Acts, who now combined with this office the newly-created position of Surveyor-General of Victualling, heartily disliked the two admirals, as well he might, for their complaints of the mismanagement of the navy were never-ending. Mr. Pepys, who had an excellent self-conceit, could be driven nearly to distraction by these two choleric gentlemen, but bearing in mind that they were apparently in favour at court, had been compelled to behave courteously to them and even provide them with wine at his own house. Now, however, he saw an opportunity to obtain revenge for the many slights which they had heaped upon his head.

"Lord, what a tale is this!" he exclaimed, when the story of the expedition into Northamptonshire was ended. "I will to the king tomorrow, and I warrant he will not be pleased."

Chubb had spread wide his hands. His Majesty already intimated that he would have no open part in the affair.

"And we have no proof that our firebrands indeed have the treasure," he added. "You may but waste your breath, Mr. Pepys."

At that, the Clerk of the Acts had laughed. He was, he said, accustomed to wasting his breath.

"Never in England has there been such a deal of breath wasted," he said. "Talk is at a premium, doctor! But his Majesty is not the man willingly to let treasure slip through his fingers. He must be told of what has happened—of what you think has happened—and perchance will take some steps. Kenton and Cocker have presumed before, but methinks never so dangerously as now. We will see . . aye, we will see."

That had been yesterday, and by this time, perchance, his Majesty had heard the tale from Mr. Pepys, though it was by no means certain that an opportunity for private audience had yet offered itself. The Clerk of the Acts prided himself that the king was friendly towards him, but Dr. Chubb knew well enough that he was but a minor official and could not approach Charles without some trouble.

"It is likely that a day or so must elapse before his Majesty hears the tale," he murmured. "And even then . . . but we must wait and see."

Tom shrugged his shoulders. His thoughts were still occupied with other matters. Wealth mattered little compared with Jennifer's safety.

"I care not," he said briefly, and then, quickly, "You must forgive me, Sam. I did not mean to be discourteous. But I . . . I have other anxieties."

He turned away from the window and crossed to the door.

"I must leave you," he said abruptly. "You will excuse me?"

He was gone on the words, leaving Chubb to

ponder, not without some jealousy, on the strange
manner in which love can alter a man. Here was
Tom Raynor, who hitherto had given no girl a
thought, obsessed by this comparative stranger. It
was an odd business, this love! He rose and walked
across to the window. Yes, there was the boy, walking up Lombard Street in the evening light, no
doubt on his way to Pudding Lane. Chubb frowned
It was, of course, unlikely that Creid would make
any further attempt to assault Jennifer, but there
was a chance that he would . . . a slight chance.

Samuel Chubb was angry with himself. He had
known that Michael Creid was not normal, and he
should have been warned in time. It was not like
him to take risks. But who would have thought that
he would so suddenly break down altogether? The
turning-point must have been the discovery that the
plague patient had died, and more horribly because
of the the plasters Creid had placed on the tokens
Creid had disobeyed orders, experimenting even
though his senior partner had forbidden it. The
discovery that his experiment had failed, and
through it the poor woman had been tortured to
death, had unhinged his brain, already weakened
That was the explanation, but it did not salve
Chubb's conscience. He should have realized that
some unexpected event might have this effect; and
he should have treated the plague patient himself
Through his laxity Creid had become insane, and
the woman had died horribly. He turned away from
the window, his face clouded.

In the meantime Tom made his way once more
towards Pudding Lane, not with any fixed inten

tion, but automatically, his feet taking him thither almost without conscious effort. As he walked his eyes scanned the faces of passers-by, searching for Dr. Michael Creid; and his imagination, always vivid, and now more so than ever, conjured up visions of the madman breaking into the Tybalds' house.

Though he was looking for Creid, it was with a shock that suddenly, as he was approaching Pudding Lane, he saw the man some twenty yards in front of him. Tom came to an abrupt halt, for Creid was standing looking down the lane. Impervious to the angry remarks of a passer-by into whom he had knocked, the boy remained motionless, watching. Creid hesitated, took a step towards the lane and then halted again. Tom's face was white as he stared at him. His hand touched the hilt of his sword. Then Creid turned abruptly and walked on, away from Pudding Lane. One glimpse Tom had of his face as he turned—pallid, the eyes wild and the lips moving silently.

Keeping some twenty yards behind him, Tom followed. The madman was now under observation, but how to apprehend him? Londoners, though eager enough to witness any unusual incident—Tom had frequently been amused since his arrival in the capital at the speed with which a crowd could gather—were also, as he knew, unwilling to take any active part in an affair which they considered none of their business. If Tom now raised the hue and cry, it was odds that Creid would make his escape while the inevitable crowd argued, some, no doubt, taking his part and demanding by what right the boy

F

attempted to restrain him. The Londoner was quick
to resent persecution, and to imagine that it existed
when in fact it did not. But something must be done.
Creid, now discovered, must not be permitted to lose
himself again amidst the crowd.

His mind working quickly, Tom followed. Creid
walked swiftly, brushing past other walkers as
though they were not there, sometimes coming into
collision with obtruding walls, but apparently
unmindful of bruises. He turned down Gracechurch
Street, right into Eastcheap and so by Cannon
Street to St. Paul's. And still Tom followed, still
he was unable to devise any plan to cope with the
present situation. If only Sam had been with him . . .

St. Paul's towered above the huddled houses
which surrounded it, a dilapidated, decayed building,
with its broken steeple—partially destroyed by fire
in 1561 and never repaired—but the hub of London,
and to the Londoner, of the universe. Its religious
significance was small compared with its social
importance. Here hucksters had set up their stalls,
within the great cathedral itself, and the aisles were
thronged from morning till night, for not only did
purchasers flock to the cathedral market, but gos-
sipers, cut-purses, touts, adventurers and all the riff-
raff of the dirty, sprawling, decaying capital made
it their headquarters. And into the cathedral turned
Michael Creid—to be lost instantly amongst the
seething mob which milled round the hucksters'
stalls.

Tom, guessing his intention too late, hurried
through the main doorway, but at once realized that
it was impossible to find his quarry. The man was

lost as effectively as though he had plunged into an impenetrable jungle. Tom plunged hopelessly through the throng, searching; but the search was hopeless, and he knew it. Creid might be anywhere in the great building—or he might have left it by another door. Tom came to a halt, condemning himself for his foolishness in allowing the madman to lose himself in this way.

Then it was, as he stood in the north aisle so helplessly, that he caught a glimpse of a familiar face. Faryner the baker was standing not two yards from him, talking, though Tom could not see his companion, for a pillar obscured his view. He moved to one side, and his eyes narrowed. The man to whom Faryner was talking was Ezekiel Hewitt, his thin, wizened face and cunning eyes easily identified. Stealthily the boy approached nearer, reached the pillar and was hidden behind it. He now stood not two feet from the men, but was entirely concealed.

The noise in the cathedral was so tremendous that it was impossible to hear more than a few isolated words spoken by Faryner and Ezekiel . . . but what he heard caused Tom's face to sharpen. Faryner was speaking.

". . . . will it be long? The trunk . . . being valuable, my house is but a poor . . . Pudding Lane is no place for it . . . the admirals . . ."

Ezekiel's reply was inaudible, but Tom had heard enough. Admirals and a valuable trunk! The treasure stolen from Bury was now in Faryner's house in Pudding Lane! Kenton and Cocker must have placed it there for greater safety. Ezekiel knew!

Faryner abruptly bade Ezekiel farewell and
moved away. Tom let him go; he was far more
interested in Ezekiel. The latter turned away from
the pillar, and as he did so a second man came up to
him. Then it was that Tom received an even greater
shock than when he had come upon Faryner and
Ezekiel. The man who was now talking in a low
voice to the latter, was none other than the vagrant
whom Tom and Chubb had befriended on the moor
near Farthingale—the man William Glover!

Tom could scarce credit his own eyes. Yet there
could be no doubt. Glover was better dressed now,
but there was no mistaking the cadaverous face, the
unusually pointed chin, the sloping forehead. This
was William Glover, the ex-sailor. Ex-sailor . . .
there, perchance, lay the connection with Ezekiel
Hewitt, who had also served in the fleet. Glover
had left the inn at Farthingale, none knew whither
or for what purpose. Hewitt had been in that neighbourhood searching for treasure; he might well have
come upon Glover at the inn, and possibly had
recruited him, either to assist him in playing a lone
hand, or into the admirals' employ.

The two men moved away. Tom plunged
into the throng, eyes strained to keep them in sight.
In this he was successful until they reached
the outer courtyard of the cathedral, and then in
the gathering gloom the quarry disappeared. For the
second time that evening Tom had failed. Twice
fortune had seemed to be on his side, but twice
she had changed her mind at the crucial moment.

He wasted no further time, but once convinced
that he had indeed lost Ezekiel and the man Glover,

made his way swiftly to Pudding Lane. His imagination, somewhat fevered, persisted in conjuring up
visions of the insane Creid seeking Jennifer, and he
condemned himself for wasting time at St. Paul's.
Once he had lost Creid he should have gone straight
to the Tybalds' house. Jennifer was of far more
importance than the treasure.

Pudding Lane was lost in black shadows. A
single lanthorn, maintained for twenty shillings a
year, bequeathed by one John Cook four years previously, was judged sufficient to illuminate the
narrow, cobbled lane.

Tom hurried down the slope towards the
Thames, in his anxiety taking no precautions against
sudden attack by cut-purses. He reached the house
he sought, to find a single window lit, and would
have gone boldly to the door and knocked had not
footsteps coming from the direction of Thames
Street stayed him. As he had done on a previous
occasion he shrank against the wall; and as before
a furtive figure approached the house and knocked
three times on the door. Tom drew in his breath
sharply. The conspirators were holding another
meeting. The Tybalds' door opened and closed
again swiftly. Tom turned into the narrow passage
between the house and the baker's shop next door.
When a meeting was in progress Jennifer was
usually sent to Faryner's house on the pretext that
the baker's wife needed her company. As Faryner
had a daughter and employed also a maid and a
man, this was obviously but an excuse.

The boy hesitated. Jennifer was probably in
Faryner's house now. He must see her, warn her

that Michael Creid was at large. He found the side-door—which corresponded to that set in the side wall of the Tybalds' house—and knocked gently. If by any ill-chance Faryner himself opened it, he could conceal himself easily enough in the inky darkness. Pressed against the wooden wall, which like the other structures in Pudding Lane was coated with pitch, he waited breathlessly. It seemed a long time. Was Jennifer in the house . . . or had some terrible tragedy already happened? Later he was to laugh at his fears, but now they were very real.

At last there came the sounds of movement from within Faryner's house.

"Who is there?"

The walls were thin, and Jennifer's voice was plainly audible, as though she were standing next to him.

"It is I, Tom."

He could hear her draw in her breath. Then the door was cautiously opened and he slipped inside. She was carrying a candle, set in a clumsy candle-stick. By its dim light the girl's face showed pale. They did not say anything for a moment, but clung to each other. Then she spoke.

"Tom, what do you here?"

Quickly and quietly he explained, telling her of Creid, of his failure to return to Lombard Street, of how he himself had seen him and then lost him.

"I was anxious for you," he said.

She smiled quickly, but her face grew serious again on the instant.

"He has not been here," she said. "Tom . . . they meet again, tonight."

He nodded, and then his eyes went along the narrow corridor in which they stood, towards the door set in the other end.

"You are not alone?"

"No. Mrs. Faryner is in the parlour, but she dozes."

"And the others?"

Her eyes were wide and frightened as she answered. No definite danger threatened, but it was as though her instinct warned her of danger. He, too, was conscious of a strange tenseness. She whispered that the two servants were in the bake-house, at the back of the premises. Faryner's daughter was in the kitchen.

"But you must not stay, sweetheart," she said.

Even as she spoke there came the noise of a door opening and closing. Jennifer's grip tightened on Tom's arm. Footsteps crossing the cobbled passageway between the two houses grated on their ears. The girl looked round wildly. Somebody was coming from Tybald's house to the baker's shop. Escape by the way Tom had come was impossible.

"Quick, up the stairs," she breathed, and pushed him towards the door at the end of the corridor.

Barely were they through it before the side door opened and they could hear the heavy footsteps inside the house.

"'Tis Faryner," she breathed in the boy's ear. "Up the stairs. There is a room on the right."

He climbed the steep stairs quickly but noise-lessly. Jennifer turned back to greet Faryner, slipping into the corridor and closing the door behind her to give Tom opportunity to reach the first floor unperceived.

Arrived at the top he found himself on a narrow landing. On his right was a door, which when he tried to open it would not move. He turned and set his hand on the latch of a second door, facing the first. It, too, was barred. As he wheeled round again a sudden light flashed on at the foot of the stairs and Faryner's huge bulk stumbled up.

"Halloa, there, who goes?"

The baker thrust Jennifer aside and lumbered up the stairs. There was no room to manœuvre, and Tom set his shoulders against the door which he had tried to open first. He heaved and the wood shuddered, creaked—and gave way. Tom stumbled into a small room, fell over a trunk lying in the middle of the floor, tried to recover himself and was crouching on one knee when Faryner threw himself upon him.

The fight was quickly over, for Faryner was a man of immense strength, and Tom, though wiry, was some four stone the lighter. He was at a further disadvantage being on one knee when the assault was launched. Faryner gripped his throat, shook him like a rat, and flung him down again. Tom's head hit against the trunk and his senses swam.

Jennifer, by now standing on the threshold, candle in hand, cried out.

"'Tis Mr. Raynor," she said. "He is no thief!"

Faryner rose to his feet, breathing fast, and stared down at the boy.

"No thief, but spy, perchance," he growled. Then

swiftly he reached for rope lying coiled in a corner of the room and fell to binding Tom's arms and legs. The girl ran to him but was pushed roughly away.

"So, he may stay until . . ."

The baker did not conclude the sentence, but picking the boy up without effort dragged him out of the room, and despite Jennifer's protests unlocked the door of the second room and flung him inside. Then he locked the door again.

"'Twas fortunate I returned," he growled. "And now, mistress, we will return to your father's house." His little eyes narrowed as he stared at her suspiciously. Then his hand came out and gripped her arm until she cried out. "What know ye, eh? Sharp ears, eh, mistress?"

"I don't know what you mean," she cried desperately. "Mr. Raynor but came to . . . to see me, and . . ."

Faryner grunted. He began to push her down the stairs.

"A likely tale," he sneered. "He came to see you, and sought you in my house? We will see what your father has to say. Likely there will be one spy less by dawn, and one more throat cut."

CHAPTER XI

In Which London's Tragedy Begins

Tom lay in acute discomfort on the bare boards of the room into which Faryner had flung him. His head ached abominably, and had bled a little where he had cut it against the sharp corner of the trunk. The ropes which bound his hands and feet cut into the flesh, torturing him. Time had lost any meaning, for he had relapsed into unconsciousness after he had been taken to the second room, recovering only to slip again into a coma. The man Faryner had used his strength brutally, and the boy's body ached and throbbed. Incoherent thoughts passed through his brain. Jennifer . . . discovered assisting him . . . the treasure, lying in the trunk in the next room . . . Jennifer . . . Creid, a madman at large . . . Faryner . . . Jennifer. Always there was Jennifer. Where was she? He groaned with pain and with the realization the girl had been taken, was in Faryner's power. He slipped back into unconsciousness.

When next he recovered his senses the chamber in which he lay was even darker. He had no idea what time it was. The house was silent, except for the scuttle of little feet as the rats explored its ancient timbers. His head still throbbed, but he felt stronger, and attempted to twist his wrists in the forlorn hope that he could loosen the rope. A sharp pain stabbed him as the cords cut even deeper, and he fell back, biting his lips. His brain, now clearer, was working feverishly. Faryner had taken Jennifer to Tybald's house, next door. How long ago?

What had happened since? The conspirators were meeting—what had they decided? To put their murder plot into immediate operation? Again he struggled desperately with the ropes. Jennifer was in danger, certainly from the conspirators, possibly also from the insane Creid; and he was helpless, trussed up like a cooking fowl, so near to the Tybalds' house; and yet for all that he could do to assist her, he might as well have been a hundred miles away.

His struggles stopped suddenly. From outside the room could be heard the creak of decaying wooden stairs. Somebody was climbing the staircase, furtively, slowly. Tom lay motionless, listening. Who was coming? And for what purpose? Faryner, come to dispatch him, quietly and without fuss? If so it seemed strange that in his own house he should walk so furtively.

Whoever it was had reached the head of the staircase, was coming towards the room in which Tom lay. The footsteps halted; a key was turned in the lock and the door slowly opened. Tom, lying on the floor in the pitch blackness, unrelieved even when the door swung open, nonetheless knew that it was Jennifer standing on the threshold. The faint perfume which was hers came plainly to him.

"Tom . . . Tom, are you there?"

He answered quietly, and the next moment she was by his side, fumbling for his wrists. He felt the cold steel of a knife touch his flesh, and then suddenly the ropes parted and he was free. Next his ankles were released and he staggered to his feet, biting his lips to restrain the cry which the pain occasioned by the sudden surge of blood through restricted veins would otherwise have brought.

Jennifer was clinging to him.

"My dear, are you hurt? Thank God I have found you. I thought . . . I thought you might be dead."

His arm went round her as he soothed her.

"I am not so easily killed," he murmured. "But how did you . . . ?"

"It was simple. They shut me in my chamber, but I escaped. It doesn't matter. Tom, you must get away. If Faryner returns . . ."

They both froze into silence as a sudden commotion broke out below. Men's voices were raised, there was the noise of wheels on cobbles, of horses stamping. Then came the sound of a door being opened and slammed shut again—then voices within the house, clearly audible and identifiable.

"Fool," quoth one voice, "besotted fool! Would you tell all London that you have our property in your keeping?"

Toms' hand gripped Jennifer's arm. The voice was that of Admiral Kenton. His reference to the treasure trunk was plain. Faryner's voice, as he answered, was no longer arrogant, but cringing.

"Your honour, I thought the man Hewitt was in your confidence. 'Twas but . . ."

Cocker broke in, angrily.

"You thought! Egad, you cannot think, rogue, for you have no mind! Bring us the trunk. Nay, we will come ourselves."

Tom and the girl shrank back against the wall of their small chamber as heavy footsteps ascended the staircase. A light showed under the door, as candles were brought. Scarcely daring to breathe the girl and the boy remained motionless. If Faryner took it into his head to open the door and inspect his prisoner, then all was lost.

The footsteps halted in the passage—and the door of the second room was flung open. Faryner was whining excuses, bringing forward in his own defence the fact that after speaking with Ezekiel at St. Paul's he had informed the admirals of what had happened.

"I left a message for your honours at Mark Lane," he muttered, "upon discovering that Hewitt no longer served you."

Kenton grunted, and swore fluently. Though Tom could not see the participants in this scene he could visualize Kenton's choleric, angry face, Cocker's chubby features suffused with rage, and Faryner's cringing. The admirals were evidently not interested in the fact that Faryner had warned them of his indiscretion at St. Paul's, but only in removing the trunk from Pudding Lane.

"Get it moved," rasped Kenton. "Take it to the coach." Then, shouting down the stairs, "Rumbold, come hither. Clewitt, be on your guard."

More footsteps ascended the staircase, and evidently the burly Rumbold lent his assistance in moving the trunk, for there came the noise of a heavy object being moved. The stairs creaked and groaned as it was transported, and then the admirals and Faryner descended once more. Tom breathed a sigh

of relief. For the moment he and the girl were safe
. . . unless Faryner took it into his head to come back
when the admirals had gone.

"Not yet," he murmured, as Jennifer moved and
began to speak. "Not yet."

And so they continued to wait in silence, until
at length they heard the coach move away, and
Faryner's footsteps, on the cobbles of Pudding
Lane, go towards Tybald's house. Silence descended
on the baker's shop. The other occupants, evidently
not unaccustomed to strange activities after dark,
had made no move, and the house might have been
deserted.

Then Tom turned to the girl.

"We must go," he said. "What o'clock is it?"

It was nearly two hours past midnight, she
thought, and in her father's house the meeting of
the conspirators still continued. She had heard
little of the proceedings, for she had been sent to
Faryner's house as soon as the meeting had com-
menced, and on her return in the baker's custody
had been afforded no opportunity to eavesdrop. Her
father had ordered her to her chamber, sternly
repressing any discussion while she was in the room
used for the meeting, and resisting Faryner's suggestion that she should be forced to tell what she
knew.

"I will speak with her myself, later," he had
said. "As for the young man, Raynor, we will discuss
him presently. Now go to your room, daughter."

Jennifer had obeyed, going to her chamber, the
door of which was locked on her. From below she
had heard the vague noise of what had sounded like

an acrimonious discussion, but had not been able to distinguish words or sentences. She had escaped from her room by climbing through the narrow window and descending to the ground by means of the sloping roof of an outbuilding.

Tom drew her to him. He had much to be grateful for. That this mere slip of a girl should have taken such a risk for him was proof enough that she loved him—and he felt both humble and proud.

"You did not see anything of Creid?" he asked.

She shook her head. Tybald, Faryner and two other men had been present at the meeting, but not Michael Creid. If he ever had been implicated in the conspiracy, which was by no means certain, she had never seen him at the house when a meeting was imminent.

"What shall we do, Tom?"

He shook his head. Little could be done but escape from this house, and from Pudding Lane. Jennifer must return with him to Lombard Street, where Sam would give her shelter. For the future? It was impossible to forecast events. Perchance nothing would come of the conspiracy, now that Tybald realized that his daughter knew or suspected what was afoot; now that it was known that Tom Raynor must also be aware of it. At all events, nothing but flight would now serve. Tybald might well make trouble when he discovered that Jennifer had fled, when he learned, as he must eventually learn, that she had gone to Lombard Street. But such matters must be left for the future. As for the treasure which Faryner, disturbed by the admirals, had handed over, that now mattered little. It was gone, almost certainly beyond recall, but it was of little significance compared with Jennifer's safety.

"We must go," he said in answer to her question. "The doctor will give you shelter, my sweet, for the time being. Come."

Together they crept down the stairs, their hearts in their mouths lest any in the quiet house should suddenly appear. Tom's head was still aching, and his body was bruised, but he was now scarcely aware of his injuries. His arm round Jennifer's shoulders he guided her down the stairs, along the short passage and so at last to the outer air.

It was a hot night, though a north-east wind had sprung up, blowing from Pudding Lane towards the Thames, affording some relief from the heat. Later this same wind was to prove a curse rather than a blessing. London lay sleeping, uneasily for the most part, for the heat of the day had been extreme, September having come in blazing. The neighbourhood of Pudding Lane was fœtid and over-crowded, the narrow, twisting streets stretching to the river, houses giving way to sheds and warehouses stored with tallow, oil, spirits and hemp. On open wharves about London Bridge lay heaps of hay, timber and coal; the timbers of houses and sheds were drought-dry, pitch-covered. And over all the heat lay close. In tiny garrets men and women lay, tossing uneasily in the heat, little guessing what catastrophe was to come to the city before morning. It was Sunday morning, and after a busy Saturday the citizens slept, weary.

As Tom and Jennifer came out of Faryner's

house, the clock of St. Magnus the Martyr, by the bridge, struck two. Tom's hand was firm on the girl's arm.

"Have no fear, sweetheart," he whispered. "You are safe now."

The words were scarce out of his mouth before the side-door of William Tybald's house was flung suddenly open, and a dim light streamed out. Jennifer and Tom were but five yards from it, having just stepped through Faryner's side-door, and no opportunity to escape into Pudding Lane was afforded. Swiftly Tom jerked the girl round and they fled down the passageway towards the back of the baker's shop. As they did so men came running out of Tybald's house, one in the lead, his voice upraised. Behind him came others.

"The evil city shall perish, for thus saith the Lord our God! Babylon, that great city, is fallen, and fire hath consumed her bones!"

The first man was calling aloud, his voice frenzied, and Tom knew that it was Michael Creid, who must have entered Tybald's house after Jennifer had left. As the fugitives reached the corner of the baker's shop, Creid suddenly wheeled, turned away from the side-door and ran in the same direction. Those behind him followed.

Events were moving so fast that it was impossible to plan ahead. The saints knew what was the meaning of this commotion, though it seemed likely that Creid, coming to Pudding Lane, had forced his way into Tybald's house and had there become frenzied. No doubt Tybald and his friends were attempting to capture the madman and restrain him. Tom, however, cared nothing for this. His one object was to escape with Jennifer. They flung themselves round the corner of the shop, at the rear, and stumbled over a pile of bavins in the tiny yard. These brushwood bundles Faryner had evidently put out ready to kindle the fire in his oven. Jennifer spoke urgently.

"There is no way out," she gasped. "Quick, in here."

In the darkness, however, she made a mistake, and the door she flung open did not lead into the store-shed, as she had supposed, but into Faryner's bakehouse. But there was no time to turn back, and before Tom could shut the door, Creid himself was upon them. He flung himself against Tom with a maniac's strength, and threw him to one side. Then he was in the bakehouse, and the men following were on his heels. In the space of seconds the place was filled. Creid was still shouting, and to Tom's ears came snatches of the Scriptures, interspersed with wild singing.

In the darkness not seeing Tom or the girl, the pursuers crowded into the bakehouse. Foremost was Faryner himself, identified by his voice as he shouted at Creid. With him was William Tybald, whose quieter voice could be heard when Faryner paused for breath. Tom, by the wall, could have touched either man merely by stretching out his hand. Next to him Jennifer was leaning against the wall, her breath coming in great gasps. Tom could feel her trembling. His hand went out to feel the frame of the door. He began to edge towards it, when suddenly a light flared up as yet another man ran across the yard with a flaming torch in his hand. Tom shrank back. Escape was cut off.

The man bearing the torch came through the doorway, and the bakehouse was illuminated. It was a macabre scene which met Tom's eyes. The great baker's oven loomed dim in one corner, a pile of faggots for relighting the fire stacked next to it. Hanging from the ceiling nearby were some flitches of bacon. By the oven stood Michael Creid, his arms flung wide, at bay before the menace represented by Faryner, Tybald and two other men, one of whom held the blazing torch; and yet though at bay, in some strange way dominating the bakehouse.

Faryner and Tybald faced him, the former threatening, a cudgel in his hand, no doubt snatched up hurriedly in Tybald's house. The latter, a few paces behind Faryner, was attempting to placate the madman. The two other men, both unknown to Tom, though he could recognize the descriptions Jennifer had previously given of the other conspirators, were taking a less active part in the affair. He with the torch was standing by the door, blocking Tom's way of escape; the other, a short sword drawn, stood between Tybald and the door. Thus. for a breathless moment they held their positions; a momentary silence had fallen. Then Creid started to rave again.

"Ye evil city, by fire shall ye perish, yea, ye and all your children, that the Lord God may ..."

His voice was drowned as Faryner raised his voice in a bull-like roar.

"Have done, fool!"

As he lifted the cudgel threateningly, and took

a step forward, the man with the torch cried out. For the first time he had become aware of the presence of Tom and the girl. Hitherto they had been in the shadows, unperceived, but as the torch was moved the dim light fell on them.

"What have we here, by the saints?"

Tybald and Faryner spun round, but before either could take action, Creid had moved. For the first time Tom saw that in his hand he held some object. Now, as he raised that hand even higher, the boy could see that he grasped an object not unlike a tennis-ball, roughly round and of about the same size.

"Ye shall all die," he shrieked, "yea, your flesh shall cringe before the flames, for thus saith the Lord!"

Swinging round he fumbled with the great iron door of the oven, seeking to undo the latches. Faryner flung himself upon him, and there was a furious struggle. Though the baker was a huge man and powerful, Creid possessed a madman's strength, and fought as a maniac will, using hands, feet and teeth, scratching and even biting. The round object fell from his hand and rolled against the oven. Then, with a superhuman effort Creid flung Faryner from him, so that the man reeled back, knocking into Tybald. The madman's voice rose in a shriek of triumph.

"Ye would kill the evil man, but ye are but poor tools in the hand of the Lord. Your courage fails, but mine comes from the Lord and He is mighty! See then, the triumph of the Lord of Hosts, who uses his poor servant that His righteousness may be apparent! Ye would kill one, but I will kill a thousand, yea, ten thousand shall perish!"

The burly Faryner, staggering to his feet, moved back a few paces. The rest gazed at the madman awestruck. It was with a physical effort that Tom wrenched himself free from the spell which Creid, in his ecstasy of madness, had woven. Faryner, Tybald and the other two men had momentarily forgotten that the boy and girl were present. Creid flung open the oven door, bent and picked up the small object, and as the door swung wide, revealing the dull red embers of a fire not yet completely drawn, threw it amongst them.

Instantly there was a blaze of light. A flame sprang from the oven, a great tongue of fire, first white and then red, which reached out towards the group so that they started back. It licked round the dry wood of the wall which stood near the oven, and almost at once there was a crackling noise, terrible to hear, as the fire surged up the wall.

For an instant none moved in the bakehouse. The course of events was so sudden, so unexpected, so devastating, that the power of movement seemed to have deserted them all. Then, as the bakehouse wall blazed along its whole length, they cowered away. The small room was built all of wood and plaster, as dry as a bone, and the flames, feeding hungrily on it, as a starving man will fasten on food, roared victoriously, fanned by the draught from the open door. To Tom, who had never seen a fire in London, it was incredible that in the space of moments the bakehouse could have been turned into an inferno. But thus it was, and Faryner, who in his years in London had witnessed many fires, for in the summer it was a common enough event in this warren of mean, dangerous streets near the Thames, knew that nothing could save his house.

As the power of movement returned to Tom, he grasped Jennifer and pushed through into the yard, nobody hindering him, for all were fully occupied. The baker sprang in fury at Creid, unheedful of his own danger. His great hands grasped the young man's throat, Creid standing now mute and apparently dazed, and flung him down . . . down towards the oven, where the pitch-ball which had been thrown amongst the embers still hissed and blazed, though it mattered little that it still burned, for the damage had been done and the blazing oven was but a small part of the roaring inferno which had been the bakehouse.

Even as Tom gained the outer air, pushing Jennifer before him, there came a shriek from behind him, and turning, he saw Michael Creid a flaming, human torch, lying on the floor. Tom drew in his breath and turned away, sick and shaking. The madman had wrought terribly—even more terribly than any yet knew—but such a death was beyond any man's deserts.

Tom caught Jennifer by the shoulder and swung her across the yard, towards the narrow passageway between the two houses. By this time flames were reaching up above the bakehouse, and out to lick the timbers of the house itself. As they ran across the yard, sparks and pieces of burning wood fell on Tom and the girl, and one such fragment, falling amongst the bavins, found there food for its hunger. The pile began to blaze.

"To Lombard Street!" gasped Tom, and as he ran could even feel some gratitude that Creid should have fired the house, for it had made possible their escape. Faryner and the others had made no attempt to follow, but were now shouting to the inmates of the building, striving to awaken them to their danger. From other houses along Pudding Lane windows and doors were banging as the residents awoke and shouted enquiries. In a matter of moments the whole lane was in a turmoil.

Tom and Jennifer came out into the lane and were nearly knocked over by men who ran, pushing and jostling, shouting and cursing. Tom drew the girl behind him, to let the men pass, but when he did venture into the lane it was to knock against two others.

He fell back, but one of the men halted, and his hand went to the belt at his waist. His lips drew back, to reveal broken yellow teeth, and before Tom could take any measures to defend himself he was upon the boy. The yellow-red light of the flames, which now had a firm hold on the whole of Faryner's house, revealed the features of Ezekiel Hewitt. With him was another man, and even as Tom fell, Ezekiel's dagger sharp at his throat, he caught a glimpse of the face of the vagrant, William Glover, befriended near Farthingale.

The attack was so sudden, so unexpected, that Tom was unable to defend himself. His head still ached, and his bruised body throbbed. A stab of pain shot through him as he fell against the side

of the house, already hot, and he was dimly aware
that he had been wounded. His senses reeled. Behind
him he heard Jennifer scream, then as through a
mist he saw Ezekiel's hand raised again, the steel
of the dagger glinting. . . . Great waves of heat were
surging from the burning house, billows of smoke
were drifting riverwards as the wind which was to
prove London's doom, blew strongly. Then Tom
was down, striking his head on the cobbles of
Pudding Lane, and oblivion closed down on him.

CHAPTER XII

In Which the Wrath of God Descends

TOM recovered consciousness slowly, and lay blinking round him at the familiar surroundings. Familiar and yet unfamiliar. This was the bed-chamber in the Lombard Street house, which he had come to know so well. He was abed in Samuel Chubb's house—as he should be. And yet . . . his hand went to his aching head, and memory came flooding back. Lombard Street . . . he should not be here. He had gone to Pudding Lane, Faryner had attacked him . . . Creid, yes, Creid had fired the baker's shop, and . . . Ezekiel, Ezekiel Hewitt had used a dagger on him. There was a sharp pain in his side. He groaned, and even as Dr. Samuel Chubb moved to the bed relapsed once more into a coma.

Yet this was not so deep as that in which he had lain for so long. His brain was awake, and through his mind passed fitful, incoherent fancies. Ezekiel . . . he had stabbed him. The dagger had been sharp . . . and the man Glover, he had been there. Fire . . . scorching, searing flames, and Jennifer. . . .

"Jennifer!"

He started up in bed again, once more conscious. Jennifer . . . the fire, caught, trapped . . . where was she?

"Quiet, lad, quiet."

A soft voice spoke, a soothing hand pressed him back on to the bed.

"You must rest, Tom. Here, drink this."

A cup was pressed to his lips, and he drank, at first slowly, but then greedily, until the sweet-tasting liquid was removed. Then the boy sank back again, and his glance, now less fevered, fell on Dr. Chubb.

"How—how did I get here?" he asked. "It was at Faryner's. The rogue Hewitt attacked me."

Sam raised his eyebrows. He had no knowledge of this. Growing anxious at the boy's prolonged absence, he had taken a servant and had made his way to Pudding Lane, arriving there to find the street in an uproar, and the baker's shop in flames.

"We found you lying near the corner of the shop," said Sam, "and 'twas a merciful providence that led us thither, for you would perchance have been trampled to death in another instant."

Tom was feeling stronger with every passing minute.

And then, as he realized that the fire might have caught Jennifer, jerked upright again. "Sam—what of Jennifer?"

The doctor was soothing again. He knew nothing of the girl, for he had not seen her, but he could assure him that she had not been burned in the fire. All the Faryner household had escaped, with the exception of the maidservant, who had been caught in a garret and had been burned to death.

"All is well, lad. The girl must have returned to her father's house and by now has escaped, I have no doubt."

"Escaped?"

Chubb bit his lip, for he had not intended this remark. Tom Raynor was in love, and he was a sick man. Let him but suspect that the whole of the Pudding Lane area was aflame, and he would be off there again, seeking his love. It was by now four o'clock on the Sunday afternoon, fourteen hours since the fire had first broken out at Faryner's shop, and by now it was becoming evident that this was no ordinary, localized fire, such as London had seen often enough in the past, but something far graver. Here, perchance, was the very fire which Mother Shipton had prophesied would destroy the capital, and of which other fanatical seers had raved even during the last twelve months.

The fire, started at the shop, had spread, to Tybald's house next-door, and then across to the Star Inn on Fish Street Hill. Flying sparks had caught the hay stored in the yard, and within moments the tavern itself was aflame. The wind had fanned the flames, the dry timber, mostly pitch-covered, of the houses in Pudding Lane and Fish Street Hill, had greatly assisted, and the fire had made progress down towards the river, laying hold on the bridge itself.

By the morning London Bridge was burning at its northern end, and St. Magnus Church had flamed, the fire eating its way to the church in parallel lines down Pudding Lane and Fish Street Hill. For the first time, at about eleven o'clock on Sunday morning, Londoners realized that the very city might be in peril, and panic broke out. Men tried desperately to rescue their goods, and the first tardy measures were taken to hinder the flames. These, however, were as yet not very effective, and the fire was making havoc in the rookery of warehouses, sheds and decaying houses clustered round the Thames.

All this Chubb knew, for from time to time as he sat with Tom in the bedchamber, word had come to him of the progress of the fire. He had not intended, however, to allow the lad to know that the Pudding Lane area—and the lane itself from Faryner's to Thames Street—was devastated. It was too late to recant now, for Tom had seized on his last remark and could not be gainsaid.

"Escaped, say you? What do you mean, Sam?"

The doctor sighed, but the damage being done, there was no way but to tell the truth. Briefly he explained the facts as far as he knew them, and though he did not exaggerate, neither did he minimize, for he could see that the boy was in no mood to be thwarted.

"But you may rest easily," he said finally. "The Tybalds must have escaped, for Faryner's house burned near an hour before any other caught."

Tom glared at him and then, before Sam could prevent him, swung out of bed. He stood swaying for a few moments, and Chubb sprang to his feet and held him.

"What madness is this?" he growled. "An you wish to die, you can seek no easier way!"

Tom pushed him aside. His side was dressed but beyond one sharp stab of pain as he first moved, the wound, evidently inflicted by Ezekiel's dagger, did not pain him greatly. His head was swimming, but with every moment he felt stronger.

"Have done," he muttered. "I go to Pudding Lane, and neither you nor any other man shall stop me. Stand back, Sam."

The doctor groaned. It was true that the wound was comparatively slight, but Tom was weak, and should rest in bed for at least another day. He did his duty and argued, but he might as well have spoken to a stone wall. The boy was impervious to all argument. Jennifer Tybald might have escaped the flames; she might have come unscathed through the rioting which must inevitably have broken out in that quarter of London upon the heels of a fire, but none knew for certain whether she had indeed escaped. Tom was going back to Pudding Lane, and only sheer inability to move would prevent him. The fire itself was not the only menace. The girl was surrounded by rogues. Creid, the madman, was dead, burned horribly, but Faryner, upon Sam's own showing, was alive, and the fanatical Tybald might not have abandoned his murderous designs. And what of Ezekiel Hewitt and the vagrant Glover, so strangely come together, both last seen in Pudding Lane?

"I go to her, by the saints!" gritted Tom. He began to dress, and eventually Sam assisted him, though his professional conscience cried out against the madness. Yet unless he manhandled the boy and forcibly flung him back to bed, he could not prevent his going. And he was forced to admit that Tom was less weak than he had supposed, and seemed in no pain, though perchance love bore him up.

"You are very fool," he said grimly, "but if you go to Pudding Lane, then I come with you."

Tom smiled, though with an effort.

"Very fool?" he murmured. "Yet you came seeking me, and grateful am I that you did."

"Aye, but I knew that you were likely enough in the lane," replied Sam. "This is but a wild goose chase. You cannot know that Jennifer is still in London."

Tom slowly buckled on his sword-belt before he answered.

"You need not be anxious, Sam. I am young and strong. Stronger than you think, perchance. And now, let us go."

Still grumbling, but realizing that he could do nothing but accompany the boy, Sam called for his burly servant, Figg, who had already once followed him to Pudding Lane, and presently the trio left the house.

"'Tis likely that you will take a fever and die," muttered Sam, as the door closed behind them.

"Nay, not die, Sam, for you can practise your skill upon me! But come, let us not delay."

So far the fire had spread towards the river, leaving the city itself untouched, but even here there was panic and confusion, men and women throwing their goods from windows, piling them into carts and pushing them away towards Moorfields. Wealthy merchants, eager to save their wealth, were loading their portable belongings into coaches, and everywhere there was confusion and terror. Down by the side of Thames it was as though hell itself had been let loose.

From the wharves men were throwing goods wildly into the river; boats, already overcrowded, were pushing off, many of them capsizing in midstream. The fire, spreading quickly along the waterfront, was red, yellow and white, according to the food it had to feed upon, and over all there was the noisome black pall of the smoke, with men appearing and disappearing in the light of the flames like very devils from hell.

To add to the horror and confusion, the rumour had quickly spread that the Papist, the Dutch and the French had fired London as revenge for the firing of the merchantmen off the Dutch coast, and the citizens, mad with terror, had turned upon all foreigners. As Tom and Sam and Figg fought their way towards Pudding Lane, a mob of men and women ran screaming towards them, on the heels of two Frenchmen, and catching them only a few yards from where Tom stood, retreating against a wall, did them to death before his very eyes. He would have started forward, but Sam pulled him back.

"Have done," he said. "You can achieve nothing."

This was true enough, for the mob was out of all control, and would as willingly have turned on the three witnesses as upon any foreigner. Tom shuddered, horrified at the spectacle of the Frenchmen lying in their own blood, felled by the leader of the mob, a blacksmith, their skulls crushed by the great iron bar he had wielded. Then Tom turned away. On, on to Pudding Lane. His blood ran cold at the thought of Jennifer Tybald caught in such a mob as this. Many were genuinely panic-

stricken and knew not what they did, but others
were eager to take advantage of the catastrophe,
and extensive looting had broken out, men risking
their lives, not to save goods from the fire but to
snatch them away before the flames denied them
plunder. Others, bestial in their cups, for the taverns
had been broken open and wine had flowed freely,
killed for the sheer pleasure of killing, and grew even
more maddened as they shed innocent blood.

At last the trio fought their way through to
Pudding Lane. Tom was unmindful of the wound
in his side, unmindful of everything but that he
must reach Pudding Lane, lest Jennifer should
yet be there.

As they reached the end of the lane, a sudden
shouting, plainly heard above the din, reached their
ears. For a moment they halted, and then Sam
grasped the boy's arm.

"Look, the fire comes back!" he gasped.

Scarce had the words left his lips before a burly
man, blundering into them, jerked out the same
warning.

"Mother of God, it fights the very wind!" he
gasped. "It comes back, back from the bridge!"

He was right. The fire was retracing its steps,
and though the wind was still blowing towards the
river, in the narrow lanes which ran down the hill
from the city to the Thames, the wind had no direction, but blew from all sides. In giant strides the
flames were coming back up Pudding Lane. The
steeple of St. Laurence Pountney was alight, and
the pitch on the houses was melting before men's
very eyes. Aye, it was coming back, back from the

bridge; back towards the eastern fringe of the city!

In Pudding Lane the residents of those houses at the top end, which had been untouched, had evidently considered that some special providence was guarding them, for unlike the merchants of the city itself, which was apparently in less danger than the upper part of Pudding Lane, they had made no move to evacuate or to move their goods. They had stood in groups watching the flames near the bridge; they had watched awestruck while Coldharbour's evil alleys had been devastated, while the Church of Allhallows-the-Less had been destroyed, the flames crashing through it as though it had been built of matchwood. They had watched their neighbours of the waterfront, less fortunate than they themselves, strive to rescue their goods—and they had helped or pillaged according to their natures. But they had not believed that the fire would come back and threaten their own houses.

Now, as they realized that the flames were advancing upon them, and that the progress of the fire was giant, they flung themselves into their decaying shops and houses and threw their goods wildly from the windows. Uproar broke out greater even than that which had previously raged, and Tom and Sam found themselves hemmed in, at first unable to move, and then swept along by the mob, swept along away from the river.

Tom struck out blindly. His head was dazed, for his strength was less than he had pretended, and he was near mad with fear for Jennifer. If the girl had left the neighbourhood, where could she have gone?

G

What protection was there for a maid caught in such a maelstrom as this? All over the city, no doubt, such mobs were seething. Again he struck out, striving to fight against the terrible current—and then, suddenly before him, not a yard away, was Jennifer. Jennifer, her gown torn and dirty, her hair dishevelled, and great streaks of soot despoiling her skin. As Tom fought his way towards her, calling her name, a man next to her caught her arm and forced her round. It was William Glover.

She saw Tom and called, but he brushed past her, intent on settling scores with the man Glover, whom he had last seen by Faryner's house, in company with Ezekiel Hewitt. As he pushed towards him, her hands came out and caught desperately at his arm.

"Tom! . . . Tom!" And then, seeing his intention, her voice rose. "Nay, he is a friend! He brought me from the fire!"

The boy hesitated and Glover broke in, struggling against the flow of the crowd.

"Not here," he muttered, and began to fight his way to the edge of the lane, where the crowd thinned. Somehow they reached the comparative safety of the nearest wall, and found a narrow passageway between the first and second houses in Pudding Lane. The throng milled past, shouting, cursing, screaming, but in the passageway all was quiet. Chubb and his servant saw them and managed to reach them.

"Well, what have you to say?" enquired Tom grimly, facing Glover, his hand on his sword-hilt.

It was the girl who answered, clinging to his arm.

"There is only this to say. He saved my life. We took refuge with a neighbour, and then the fire came back, when none expected it, and he brought me out. Tom, last night, he did not know what Hewitt intended. Had it not been for him Hewitt would have killed you."

Tom's grim face relaxed a trifle, but he still glared at Glover straightly. The man spoke quietly.

"She speaks truth, master. I served with Hewitt in the fleet, but knew not that he had a quarrel with you. He offered me work in London and I came. Think you I would injure the friend of the man who saved my child's life?"

The man's voice carried conviction, and Tom's hand fell away from his sword.

"What of Hewitt?" he asked.

Glover shrugged his shoulders. On the previous night he had not been able to prevent the man attacking Tom, for the assault had been made so quickly, and already Pudding Lane had been in an uproar at the first alarm of fire. But he had been able to turn the second dagger stroke aside, and thus almost certainly had saved the boy's life. Then a press of neighbours had swept down upon them, Ezekiel Hewitt had disappeared, and Glover and the girl had been forced away from the baker's shop in the turmoil. Jennifer had been dragged away, her protests unheeded, and by the time she had been able to return, there was no sign of Tom. She had been near distracted, knowing nothing of the circumstances or that Sam had found him. The rest of the day she had spent at a neighbour's house farther up the lane, and exhausted had been sleeping when the fire burned back from the bridge and attacked the lane again.

All this she recounted in broken sentences, often the words inaudible, for the crash of falling timbers was growing nearer, and the din of the crowd rose to a crescendo. It was evident that she was near to fainting. Chubb pushed forward.

"We must take her away from this," he said. "Figg, go before, and we will follow."

They turned and stood at the mouth of the passageway, awaiting an opportunity to enter the lane itself. Figg, burly and apparently unmoved by the turmoil, was in front, with Tom and Chubb on either side of Jennifer. Behind came Glover. As they waited, Tom turned to him.

"What of Tybald?" he asked.

Glover glanced at Jennifer, and when he answered his voice was low, so that she could not hear.

"I saw him go," he said. "Nothing could be done. It was a quick death. A roof timber fell on him. She does not know yet."

Tom nodded, but his arm tightened round her shoulders. Tragedy had come swiftly upon London, and upon countless of her citizens. Men and women had died horribly in the flames, and many more would go to their ends before the fire had burned itself out. Buildings could be cleared and rebuilt; human lives could not be. William Tybald had gone to his account, and eventually his daughter must know of it. But not yet. She was exhausted, swaying as she stood waiting. More she could not endure until she had rested. As he tightened his arm round her, Tom Raynor's heart was full of gratitude that he had come to Pudding Lane. He turned to Glover again.

"I misjudged you," he said quietly. "You have my gratitude for what you have done."

"It was little enough," was the slow answer. "Had I known that Hewitt had a quarrel with you, I would not have come to London. But he offered me gold."

There came a slight lessening in the seething mob passing along the lane, and seizing the opportunity the little group left the passageway and plunged across the narrow street. They reached the other side in safety and turned towards the city, up Gracechurch Street and so into Lombard Street. Here there was confusion, though not so great as in Pudding Lane and its neighbourhood. Thinking still that the fire would burn itself out or be halted before it reached the street, men from the immediately threatened areas were bringing their goods to the houses of friends, seeking safety for chattels and families. Some merchants, more wary, were loading their goods into waggons and coaches preparatory to seeking the country districts. Thus Lombard Street was in confusion, some coming, others going.

As Tom's party came into the street, a familiar figure loomed up before them. It was Samuel Pepys, his garments dishevelled, but in some strange way giving the impression that underneath his natural fear and perturbation lurked a not unpleasurable excitement. He was watching the little goldsmith, Stokes, accepting goods from some friends, but talked eagerly to Chubb when he saw him, glad enough to be able to impart news.

"Little enough can be done," he said, "though his Majesty does all that man can do. They say he has come down the river from Whitehall and superintends the pulling down of buildings. But Lord, what fools there are! My Lord Mayor clucks like any hen, and raises helpless hands to heaven. I met him in Canning Street not an hour since, and I would to God we had a man amongst us."

He scarcely waited for Chubb to speak, but darted off, still, even in the midst of this turmoil, full of self-importance. With heavy hearts the others pushed on towards the doctor's house. A heavy pall of smoke hung over the city, shot through with flames—flames which crept ever nearer to the wealthy regions on the ridge of the hill from which Pudding Lane and the other twisting roads ran down to the river. The fires on Fish Street Hill and St. Laurence Pountney, hitherto separate, were now burning towards each other. The riverside district was devastated, though the major portion of the bridge had been saved, and now, with the fire sweeping towards the city, was apparently out of danger. Ever and anon came the noise of explosions as houses were destroyed in the path of the fire, but still there was hope that the flames would be stayed before they reached the Lombard Street district. At all events, it must be some time before the fire could attack the city itself, and Chubb considered that it was essential that both Jennifer and Tom should have rest.

He therefore turned into his house, where the servants were huddled together, watching the fire from vantage points and muttering together. Their master's arrival stirred them effectively into action, for Chubb had a commanding manner. Within a short time a chamber had been prepared for Jennifer, and after a soothing draught mixed by Chubb himself, she sought her bed. Her face was very white, and she swayed as she took her leave of Tom.

"Go and sleep, my sweet," he said gently. "And do not fear that you will be trapped again. You are well guarded."

"Yes, well guarded," she repeated, and lifted her mouth to be kissed. Then, moving away, she spoke again. For the last hours she had been moving as in a dream, content to do as she was told, her brain numb. Now, however, anxiety once more clouded her eyes. "Tom, what of my father? What has happened to him?"

The boy bit his lip, but lied smoothly. Not yet must she be called upon to face her loss.

"He is safe enough," he said. "He lost you in the crowd, but tomorrow we will find him. Now, go to your rest, Jennifer, and do not fret."

Whether he carried conviction or not he did not know, but she turned and went into her room, her face expressionless.

Tom turned away and sought his own bed. With the dangers at least temporarily overcome, reaction had set in. His whole body ached, and the dagger wound in his side was beginning to pain him again. He was scarcely conscious of the doctor helping him to undress, or of the bitter taste of the concoction held to his lips. He sank at once into a deep sleep, and watching him for a few moments Chubb was satisfied that he had taken no lasting harm from the expedition to Pudding Lane. Sam sighed as he listened to the boy's even breathing. Youth was a wonderful thing!

Outside, in the corridor, he paused and gazed out of the window which looked out towards the river. It was as though the wrath of God had indeed descended on London. The fires, many of them now united, others burning rapidly towards each other, blazed hideously, the smoke drifting in huge clouds, billowing out across the city. Chubb was no fanatic, but level-headed, yet even he saw the hand of God in this terrible destruction. Michael Creid had raved of this evil city reaching salvation only through the cleansing fire. Evil it was, in truth, for dirt and decay were evil. God had struck, not directly, perhaps, but through his creatures, burning out their pestilential warrens, cleansing the filth and disease of centuries. London burned, and her citizens suffered; but out of this catastrophe perchance good might come.

Dr. Samuel Chubb turned away from the window and went downstairs. Men said that the fire could not reach Lombard Street, but nothing was certain in this life. For the rest of the night Chubb busied himself collecting together his valuables. By daybreak it might be necessary to leave this house.

CHAPTER XIII

In Which the King has his Revenge, and Tom Raynor his Reward

TUESDAY, September 4th, 1666, had already proved, by the early evening, to be the most tragic day London had ever witnessed—and worse was to come. During the previous day the fire had progressed unhindered, destroying Baynard's Castle, surging in a great bow of fire from Blackfriars to Threadneedle Street and Leadenhall, burning fiercely about the great Stocks Market, bringing death and destruction to the narrow alleys and streets north and south of the Poultry and south of Cheapside. The north-east wind, which had shifted a point or two to the east, and was roaring and whistling through London as yet unchecked, had carried the fire first from Pudding Lane down to the river, and then, halted by the water, the flames had been driven to the centre and west of the city itself, only the fringes to the east of Pudding Lane escaping. Lombard Street had been destroyed on the previous afternoon.

Tom Raynor stood by the parlour window of a house in Bishopsgate, near Moorfields, and brooded over the city, flaming to the west; and his eyes watched the ceaseless flow of people streaming into Moorfields for refuge, their belongings piled high on carts and barrows. He would have been less than human had he not felt pity for these refugees, for the mothers, wild-eyed as they clutched their children, for the men who had seen their houses, their goods and often enough their families burned before their very eyes. He would have been less than human had he not been conscious of the strange terror—different from any other fear—bred by this vast, all-consuming fire. Since the dim ages when man first walked the earth clad in skins, fire has brought him a panic terror; in London on this September day it was not only the physical destruction which terrified, for at the back of men's minds lay the unreasoning, instinctive fear and horror of unquenchable fire.

Dr. Chubb's forethought in preparing his valuables for transport had been justified. The flames had spread to Gracechurch Street, and from there to wealthy Lombard Street itself. The merchants had been forced to leave their luxurious dwellings— the goldsmith Stokes, who had accepted his friends' goods on the Sunday evening, had within a few hours been compelled to transfer them elsewhere together with his own—and the Chubb household had fled before the flames. Much property, not easily transported, had been left behind, but the majority of the doctor's wealth was still safe enough, guarded by Figg and three other servants, and was now housed in this Bishopsgate residence, owned by a friend of the doctor's and put at his disposal.

Near twenty-four hours had elapsed since Tom, Jennifer and Chubb had reached the Bishopsgate house, and those hours had been tense. With the wind firmly settled in the north-east, it was extremely unlikely that the flames would reach out to Bishopsgate, lying as it did due north of Grace-church Street, but for all this assurance, the residents could find no rest. London was in a turmoil such as had never been seen before, and few sought their beds on that Monday night, even though unless the wind veered suddenly, they themselves were safe enough. The house had been awake all night, the kindly owner doing what he could to assist the never-ending stream of refugees, opening his doors to friends and strangers alike, so that the place was full to overflowing for hours on end. Meals were forgotten, until hunger forced Tom and Chubb to seek food—and then it was but a makeshift repast, eaten in the crowded parlour.

Now, during the late afternoon, Tom stood brooding by the parlour window, restless, oppressed.

He gazed out of the window, peering through the great pall of yellow smoke which was drifting menacingly over the city, and played restlessly with his sword-hilt. The king had called upon the citizens to fight the fire, and many had responded. Houses were being pulled down in the path of the flames, and the inadequate fire-fighting appliances were manned, though the conduits which fed London with water were nearly dry owing to the long drought. Little enough could be done while this cursed wind still blew strongly, but Tom itched to be out and doing, assisting to some extent to fight the fire.

As though reading his thoughts, Jennifer Tybald, sitting on a low stool behind him, spoke quietly.

"No, Tom, you must not go out. Have I not lost enough already?"

He turned swiftly and crossed to her. Yes, she had lost enough—and now knew of her loss. Tom himself had broken to her the news of her father's death, a distasteful task, but his and no other's. She had taken it bravely, quietly, and he had not seen her weep, though later there were signs of tears on her face.

"Yea, you have lost, sweetheart. I . . . I am sorry, but what are words? But you have me dearest, and always shall have, please God."

She smiled at him and pressed his hand. Silence fell, but eventually she spoke. Tom had turned back to the window.

"Tom, I spoke selfishly. You must go, if you feel you must."

Again he came to her, and his hand was gentle on her hair.

"I am strong again," he said, "and . . ."

He broke off as the door opened and Glover came in. Tom had not seen him for some hours, and it was evident from the dirt and grime on Glover's face, and from his torn garments, that he had been out in the fire-ridden districts. Unobtrusively the man had attached himself to Chubb's household, and had proved a tower of strength during the terrible hours in Lombard Street, and during the journey to Bishopsgate. It was apparent that he wished to repay, as well as he was able, Chubb's efforts on his behalf. There was no question of his loyalty. Tom's eyes were warm as he watched the man approach.

"What news?" he enquired eagerly. "You have been out?"

Glover nodded, wiping the back of his hand across his forehead.

"Aye. Cheapside is aflame from one end to the other, and St. Mary-le-Bow has gone. Guildhall has caught, and men say St. Paul's will burn."

Tom drew in his breath. He was no Londoner, but even to the countryman, with little knowledge of the capital, the thought of the great cathedral burning was tragic. It had withstood many fires, many other scourges; it was a symbol, and though despoiled by hucksters, though falling into decay, it remained a symbol. London was St. Paul's, and St. Paul's was London. It was unthinkable that any fire, however great, could bring that great structure to naught. Yet the fire was sweeping towards it, a fire such as no man had ever seen before.

Tom's hand gripped his sword-hilt tightly. Then he turned to Jennifer, who was watching him with wide eyes.

"I must go," he said briefly. "God be with you, sweet."

"And with you."

They kissed, she held him to her for a moment, and then he was gone, swiftly, with Glover at his heels. The girl remained motionless, until the door opened yet again and Chubb came in. He crossed to her.

"Take heart, child," he said softly. "No harm will come to him. But he is a man—though like all women you perchance look upon him as a child—and a man must fight or die."

He smiled down at her and she returned the smile. Yes, men were men—and children.

"I know," she said.

Out in the street, along which the refugees still streamed, Tom and Glover fought against the crowds, seeking to force a way south, towards the fire. It was no easy task, but at length they reached the junction of Bishopsgate and Cornhill, and came suddenly to the utter desolation left by the fire. Heaps of smouldering ashes lay to right and left, flames still fitfully burning amongst them. The air was dry, and the smoke rising from smouldering ruins was near suffocating. Here, at the corner, they paused, and for the first time since leaving the house, Glover spoke. His eyes turned east, towards Fenchurch Street and Mark Lane.

"There is evil work afoot," he said. "I came to fetch you, master."

"Aye, evil work," replied Tom. "We must do what we can."

Glover scowled at the blackened ruins of houses and shops.

"I speak not of the fire," he said, "but of Hewitt. He seeks Mark Lane, and what he may find there. He and others who have gathered round him."

Tom's eyes sharpened. Mark Lane, as yet untouched by the fire, which was sweeping westwards; Mark Lane, where dwelt Kenton and Cocker, whither, no doubt, they had transported the treasure which they had rescued from Pudding Lane immediately before the outbreak of the fire. The treasure . . . Tom's mind had been too full of other matters to have room for thoughts of the treasure. Once so important, it had faded into insignificance compared with the personal and national calamities which had crowded in during the last three days.

"What do you mean?" he asked. "What of Hewitt?"

"He plots murder, master. I heard him with my own ears at The Bull, not a hundred yards from here. We lay there after reaching London, and I returned thither an hour ago."

There was no time to question Glover further, but Tom had no doubt that the man was speaking the truth. The fire had proved a golden opportunity to loot and plunder, and London was swarming with thieves and cut-purses, who braved the flames in order to steal. Ezekiel Hewitt would have no difficulty in recruiting rogues for his purpose. That purpose was to secure the treasure, and if necessary to murder.

"Come," said the boy. "We will to Mark Lane."

Glover said nothing, but turning, followed Tom towards Mark Lane. As they walked, as swiftly as they could, hindered by the streams of refugees, which though fewer in number here, outside the radius of the fire, on occasions blocked their passage, he briefly answered the boy's questions.

He had returned to The Bull not with the intention of seeking Ezekiel, whom he had not seen since the outbreak of the fire, but to slake his burning thirst, for he had been near the heart of the fire all morning, doing what he could to assist those who fought the flames. It had been but sheer chance that

amongst the throng which filled the inn—for your
true Londoner must drink even in the midst of
calamity—he should have seen Ezekiel. The man
had with him four rogues, who no doubt had been
active plundering the city. It had not been difficult
to overhear sufficient of the conversation to realize
that Ezekiel intended to seek Mark Lane and the
admirals' house—and to kill if any hindrance were
placed in his way.

As he and Glover turned into Mark Lane, an
open cart, piled high with goods, drove towards
them. An ill-kempt fellow with matted hair and a
patch over one eye held the reins, driving the sorry-
looking nag; two others shambled alongside. Riding
in the back of the cart was Ezekiel Hewitt, seated on
a trunk.

As the cart drew level with Tom and Glover,
Ezekiel turned, and his eyes rested on the boy. His
yellow teeth showed as he spat out a curse, and his
hand went swift to his belt, withdrawing a dagger.
Scarce had he done so before Tom was upon him,
pushing between the people, paying no heed to their
vociferous protests, and flinging himself upon the
cart. The driver, reining in instinctively, made the
task the easier. Before Ezekiel's companions well
knew what was afoot, Tom had clambered up the wheel
and was in the cart. There was neither time nor space
to draw his sword. His hand shot out and gripped
Ezekiel's wrist, and he strove desperately to twist
the dangerous dagger from his grasp. Ezekiel rose
from the trunk, thrust aside a bale of cloth, no doubt
pillaged from some burning warehouse or shop, and
gave battle.

He was small but wiry, and now fought with desperation. His lips drew back in a snarl, and his other hand came out to grip the boy's throat. He had thought to have dispatched this Raynor at Pudding Lane, yet here he was again, attempting to thwart his designs. Hewitt snarled with rage, and his knee came up suddenly, to take Tom in the stomach and send him writhing with pain to the bottom of the cart. He fell across the bale of cloth, and for a moment was helpless, the agony almost too great to bear. The blow had not contacted the recent wound in his side, but this now shot tongues of pain through his whole body, and was bleeding anew.

Ezekiel cried out in triumph. His dagger went up, and came down again like a flash of silver light. It was a miracle that it did not strike through Tom's heart. Had it not been for a sudden jerking of the horse's head, as Glover caught the driver round the waist and hurled him from the plank seat, the stroke would have found its mark. As it was the steel buried itself in the bale of cloth, and before Ezekiel could withdraw it, Glover was on him, hurling him down. Ezekiel's head hit the side of the trunk and for a moment he was stunned. The other two rogues, who during the few moments of the battle had been standing by witless, now sprang forward.

Tom, recovered, but still racked with pain, and a red mist swimming before his eyes, flung himself on them blindly, scarce knowing what he did. His grasping arms found one man's legs and the fellow fell backward off the cart, the wheel of which he had been climbing. His head thudded sickeningly on the roadway. Blood gushed from a split skull and he lay motionless. Glover, turning from Ezekiel, swept the other away with a blow, and as he did so Ezekiel, recovering, grasped the dagger and jerked it from the bale.

The crowd, pausing momentarily in its flight, crowded round the cart, shouting encouragement promiscuously, some reaching forward to snatch goods from the cart. The horse, terrified at the noise and the smell of fire and smoke, thrashed out with its forehoofs, screaming with fear. As Ezekiel grasped the dagger and raised it, jerking forward to reach Glover, whose back was now turned to him, a woman screamed, piercing, shrill. Through the red mist Tom saw the dagger raised, saw Glover's back presenting the perfect target—and desperately the boy threw himself forward. He crashed into Ezekiel, gripped his right wrist and by some miracle held on for all his fast-waning strength. Ezekiel fell again, and then, suddenly, went limp. The man whom Glover had knocked aside had recovered, had drawn his own dagger and had struck. At the vital moment Ezekiel had fallen back—and the dagger had found his ribs. He was dead within a few seconds. The man stared at him, and then, dropping the dagger, leaped from the cart and was lost amidst the crowd, which willy-nilly closed round him.

A sudden shout set the crowd seething again, withdrawing their attention from the cart and from the men who ran shouting up Mark Lane. A great finger of fire had sprung up to the west, a finger which grew larger, brighter. Then a mass of red flame surged out. St. Paul's was alight, burning along the whole length of the roof.

"'Tis Paul's!" shrieked a woman, "Paul's burns!"

It was as though this last act of destruction threatened the crowd with immediate death, though in fact the cathedral was more than a mile distant.

They milled past. Forgotten was the fight, the deaths of two men. What mattered two deaths when London was burning, when hundreds of its citizens had been burned alive, when Paul's itself was aflame? In a seething mass the crowd surged on.

Tom was lying across the treasure trunk, his breath coming in great gasps. Blood was running away from the newly-opened wound, seeping through the cloth of his clothes. The world swam before his eyes. The roar of the flames, the crash of masonry as St. Paul's crashed to ruin, clearly audible in Mark Lane, merged in the roar and beat of the blood in his own veins. Yet as he lay his hand grasped the edge of the trunk.

Glover bent over him, then straightened, threw Ezekiel's body over the edge of the cart, and as men burst through the crowd, running towards him from the admirals' house, he gathered the reins and set the horse, maddened by fear, moving into Fenchurch Street. Little enough of the plundered goods which had piled on the cart now remained, for much had been snatched by grasping hands during the fracas, and most of the remainder had fallen, to litter the cobbles of Mark Lane. But the trunk remained, with Tom Raynor huddled across it. And thus William Glover, sometime sailor, sometime vagrant, brought the cart to Bishopsgate.

.   .   .   .

The sunlight poured through the tall windows of the gallery at Whitehall, just as it had done when Tom had first had audience with the king—so long ago it seemed, though it was but a matter of a few weeks.

Whitehall, its buildings and its gardens, were untouched by the fire which had brought London down in ruins, and standing there in the gallery, before his Majesty, Tom found it difficult to realize that so near at hand London lay a mere heap of smouldering rubble. He found it difficult, too, to realize that this saturnine man, this pleasure-seeking king, had striven to stay the fire as though he were but a labourer, stripping off his coat and working in shirt-sleeves, often risking his life, exhorting the citizens to further efforts, commanding, planning, and by his skill and hard work saving something of his capital.

The fire, the fury of which had ended on Thursday, September 6th, a week ago—though even yet small fires still burned here and there, and wisps of smoke ascended from the heaps of rubble which had been houses—had wrought a havoc such as no man could have envisaged. It was still too early to compute the damage in detail, but it was estimated that at least 200 acres of the city had been devastated, that at a conservative estimate 80 parish churches had disappeared, and that near 13,000 houses had been totally destroyed. St. Paul's had crashed in ruins, the Guildhall was badly damaged, though the great walls still stood, Cheapside had been devastated, Lombard Street and Gracechurch Street destroyed . . . the list was too long to detail.

London was, literally, a heap of smouldering rubble.

Now, looking at his Majesty, Tom realized that this man, reputed pleasure-seeking with no thought in his head but how to enjoy himself, had been slandered. He was still exquisitely dressed, and his dark eyes were as sardonic as ever, with no hint of tragedy in them. Yet Tom knew, and others knew, that he had worked like a fiend to save his city. The boy realized that this sardonic, cynical humour, this apparently casual manner, must mask a sense of tragedy as deep as any man's. Charles Stuart had led a strange, tense life; it had taught him to conceal his emotions.

"So, it is over," he said abruptly, turning from the window and addressing his audience impartially. His eyes travelled from Tom Raynor to Samuel Pepys, from the Clerk of the Acts to Dr. Chubb—and lastly to Jennifer Tybald, whose copper-gold hair caught and held the sunlight as it streamed through the window. He laughed and spoke again. "I have ever been a king without money," he said. "Now am I a king without a capital city !"

"It has been a tragedy such as few nations have beheld, your Majesty," said Mr. Pepys. "This very morning I heard a country fellow declare that London now looks like his native Westmorland fells."

Charles gestured with one delicately-moulded hand—gestured helplessly.

"Yes, a tragedy," he repeated quietly, "a tragedy." Then, his mood changing, he turned to Tom. "The . . . the trunk which you conveyed hither," he said abruptly, "has been examined. You have our gratitude, Mr. Raynor. You shall have more than our gratitude." He smiled swiftly, adding, "gratitude is pleasant, but . . ." He shrugged his shoulders.

"Your Majesty, I but returned to you that which is yours," said the boy quickly. "The wealth was brought to Naseby for your martyred father's use. Now 'tis yours."

Charles looked at him with smiling eyes.

"Perchance your law is not good law," he said. " 'Tis likely that the Lord Chancellor would quarrel with you, and 'tis certain that the Commons would ! But enough of that. What I have I hold. As for you, sir, I have made arrangements to requite you. Monk's Abbey lies next to your estate at Market Stanton, I believe ? 'Tis within the gift of the crown, and shall now pass to you. The rents are substantial and will assist you, I have no doubt."

Tom stammered his thanks, but the king waved them aside.

He glanced at the girl again, and added, "You have other reward, Mr. Raynor, and perchance 'tis worth more to you than Monk's Abbey ! Nay, more than all England, I think !"

Jennifer blushed beneath the king's gaze.

"A pretty pair, your Majesty," murmured the Clerk of the Acts. And being a sentimental man, fell to wishing that he was still as young as Tom, though if all the tales told of him were true, reflected Chubb, watching him, lack of youth was no great hindrance to him !

The king did not answer, but fondled the long

ears of his favourite spaniel. When he spoke it was
apparently to the dog.

"We have other visitors expected," he murmured. "Admiral Kenton and Admiral Cocker will
be most welcome."

There was a tense—and surprised—silence.
Tom glanced in bewilderment at Chubb.

"Yes, they will be welcome," repeated Charles.

As he spoke he rose to his feet, for the door of the
gallery had swung open, and an usher announced
Kenton and Cocker. The two admirals swaggered
in, still red of face, still evidently well pleased with
themselves, though a close observer might have
discerned some anxiety in their eyes. Charles
evidently saw it, for when he welcomed them he
added his condolences that they should have been
robbed of certain of their property during the course
of the fire.

"Yes, 'twas a heavy loss, your Majesty," sighed
Kenton. "Our house was untouched, thanks be to
God, but rogues broke in on Tuesday, and made
off with valuables prepared for transport."

"You have our sympathy," replied Charles
smoothly.

Kenton and Cocker bowed, but their eyes slid
round to Tom and Chubb, and it was clear that they
were indeed worried, not only because they had
suffered loss but because for the first time it had
occurred to them that their activities at Naseby might
be known to his Majesty.

Kenton and Cocker, completely unsuspicious
when they had entered the gallery, were now
wondering whether by any strange chance this

infernal young puppy Raynor could have had any
hand in the lifting of the treasure.

Their thoughts, taking the same line, were interrupted by the king.

"Indeed you have our sympathy," he murmured
again. "And now, you must drink with us."

He clapped his hands lightly and wine was
brought—wine in silver goblets. The servant handed
one to Cocker, another to Kenton. As he did so
Kenton's eyes bulged, and Cocker's face grew even
more suffused. These goblets, these silver goblets
.... they knew them well enough, for when last they
had seen them they had been with the other plate
and gold in the trunk. The design of this pair of
drinking goblets was unusual; it was scarce possible
that ... No, by the saints, they were the same! The
delicately wrought handles, fashioned in the shape
of slim girls; the stems, rising from ornate decora-
tion ... these goblets had been discovered at
Naseby, had been stolen by Ezekiel Hewitt, and
were now in the possession of his Majesty!

"Come, sirs, drink," said Charles, and his eyes
were cold as he stared at the unhappy admirals.

With shaking hands they obeyed, but the wine
tasted sour! The king must know of their activities,
that was the thought uppermost in their minds. He
knew that they had been prevented only by chance
from defrauding him. It was not a pleasant thought.
What would he do? What penalty would be
imposed? The two admirals quaked.

There was a long silence, while Charles continued to gaze at his victims. Then a slow smile
touched his sardonic mouth.

"Think you not that the goblets are delightful?" he enquired. "They have but recently come into my possession. Perchance you would care to hear their history?"

Kenton swallowed hard. Cocker near choked over his wine. His Majesty paused before continuing.

"But no, it would probably not interest you. And now, sirs, I bid you farewell. I doubt if you will find it convenient to wait upon me again for some long time. We shall excuse your attendance."

Charles was no longer smiling. His voice was imperious. Kenton and Cocker stammered, bowed awkwardly and hurriedly departed, thankful to get away. Charles had achieved a subtle revenge, and was well content. When the admirals had departed he again addressed the spaniel.

"So, Carlos, even kings must laugh sometimes! Think you not that it was clever? I could not openly punish our firebrands, for it would not be politic to make this matter public. You agree? Yes, of course. But they knew an uncomfortable moment, I think. And they will not talk. No, they will not talk."

He fondled the dog's ears, and the animal, seeming to understand, wagged its tail.

"And now, I bid you all farewell," said Charles, turning to his audience. "You have my thanks, and my best wishes."

His visitors bowed themselves out and made their way by water back to the devastated city and so eventually to Bishopsgate, where three of them still lodged. The city smouldered yet, its ruins gaping, while amongst them flitted men and women, searching for what they might find amid the smouldering ashes.

Tom Raynor's thoughts were of Market Stanton, so fresh and sweet . . . and of Jennifer, soon to be his wife. On the morrow they would return to Oxfordshire, he and Jennifer, and Dr. Samuel Chubb. With them also would journey William Glover, who would presently be joined by his wife and child. The Glovers would not again know the pinch of poverty or be hounded from parish to parish.

That evening, the last they would spend in London, Tom and Jennifer sat in the parlour of the Bishopsgate house. Outside it was growing dark, and the room itself was but dimly lit by two candles. Tom watched the girl, watched the soft gleams in her copper-gold hair, the lovely line of her face.

"It is over," he said softly, "and . . . there is Market Stanton."

She nodded. She had been thinking of her father, of the plot which a greater evil had prevented; wondering what had happened to Faryner and the other conspirators. No mention had been made to anybody of the plot to kill the king. No doubt nothing ever would be heard of it. And she had been thinking of Michael Creid, poor unhappy Creid, in his madness responsible for London's great disaster. Had he indeed been implicated in the murder plot, or had he but returned in his madness to Pudding Lane and forced his way into the house, there to horrify the conspirators with his insane ravings? None could know except Faryner and the other two men, and they had disappeared. But it did not matter. Her father . . . he was dead, but it had been a quick, merciful death, better than the fate which might have overtaken him at the executioner's hands. She sighed, for she had loved that strange, fanatical man, William Tybald. But . . . there was Tom, and Market Stanton.

"Yes, there is Market Stanton," she said slowly. "Tom, tell me about it."

He slipped his arm round her waist, and his voice murmured on, telling her of his home, while the darkness gathered outside, and the candles burned low.